12/09

Newcastle Libraries and Information Service

☎ **0845 002 0336**

Due for return	Due for return	Due for return
− 3 JUN 2010	2 0 FEB. 2010	

Please return this item to any of Newcastle's Libraries by the last date shown above. If not requested by another customer the loan can be renewed, you can do this by phone, post or in person.
Charges may be made for late returns.

Lauren Liebenberg grew up in Rhodesia during the civil war. When still a child, she left what had become Zimbabwe, following her girlhood... [?] south, to Johannesburg, where she still lives today. She has an MBA from the University of Witwatersrand and is married with two children.

The Voluptuous Delights of Peanut Butter and Jam was short-listed for the Orange Prize for New Writers 2008.

The
Voluptuous Delights
of
Peanut Butter and Jam

LAUREN LIEBENBERG

virago

VIRAGO

First published in Great Britain in 2008 by Virago Press
This paperback edition published in 2009 by Virago Press
Reprinted 2009

A CIP catalogue record for this book
is available from the British Library.

ISBN 978-1-84408-468-5

Typeset in Caslon by M Rules
Printed and bound in Great Britain by
Clays Ltd, St Ives plc

Papers used by Virago are natural, renewable and
recyclable products sourced from well-managed forests and certified in
accordance with the rules of the Forest Stewardship Council.

Mixed Sources
Product group from well-managed
forests and other controlled sources
www.fsc.org Cert no. SGS-COC-004081
© 1996 Forest Stewardship Council
FSC

Virago Press
An imprint of
Little, Brown Book Group
100 Victoria Embankment
London EC4Y 0DY

An Hachette UK Company
www.hachette.co.uk

www.virago.co.uk

The
Voluptuous Delights
of
Peanut Butter and Jam

Acknowledgements

For taking the risk, for parting the waters, for his sheer ebullience, I am for ever grateful to Patrick Janson-Smith, my agent. The Christopher Little Agency is indeed a remarkable fraternity to which to belong.

To Lennie Goodings, my editor, for taking *Peanut Butter* where it would never have dared to venture. To all at Virago for their relentless brilliance.

To my own extraordinary and wonderful family, who are, it must be said, such fertile ground!

And to Mark, my love, who makes it possible.

Thank you.

Historical Note

The story you are about to read takes place in a dying country.

In 1965, the British colony of Southern Rhodesia, under the leadership of its prime minister, Ian Smith, made a 'unilateral declaration of independence' (UDI) to thwart the British abdication of power to black Africans. In the aftermath, the defrauded black Africans took up arms against the white rulers of the newly rechristened Rhodesia.

Two tribal factions – the northern Shona, led by Robert Mugabe, and the southern Ndebele, led by Joshua Nkomo – fought a long and bloody campaign, which became known as the 'Bush War' by white Rhodesians and as the 'Second Chimurenga' ('rebellion' in Shona – see the glossary at the end of the book) by the blacks.

The war was fomented in the crucible of the Cold War, and the freedom fighters were backed by both the People's Republic of China and the Soviet Union. Moreover, landlocked Rhodesia was besieged by hostile neighbours, especially newly independent Mozambique and Zambia. Apartheid South Africa initially allied with the Rhodesians, but later withdrew its support under international pressure, offering up Rhodesia as a 'sacrificial lamb'.

Denied any international recognition, and subject to UN sanctions from the day of its inception, Rhodesia faced a severe economic struggle during the 1970s, compounded by the conscription of all white men.

Eventually, isolated, buckling under economic pressure and faced with a growing body count, the embattled Rhodesians surrendered. A ceasefire in 1979 led to elections in 1980, which were won by Robert Mugabe's ZANU (PF), and the new state of Zimbabwe was born.

It was raining, I remember, the day he came to the Vumba, the lush rain of Africa, winged ant hatchlings swarming from the steaming earth.

Now, years later, the rain billows with my ghosts of shadow and light and sadness.

It takes me back to my forest, to the clutches of golden orb spiderlings supping from their yolk sacs on a nest of silk, to the strictured breathing of the vines as they strangle one another, to the praying mantis that delicately, greedily, feasts upon her lover as they are gripped in coitus on dripping leaves.

It was so long ago, though, and I was only a child. I wonder how much of what I remember is the truth. What I do remember is that once he came a kind of madness bloomed in our garden of innocence.

1

Cia is my sister and I am her leader. The two of us are sitting on the flagstone steps outside the kitchen door eating our peanut butter and jam sandwiches. Cia peels hers apart, as she always does, and slowly licks out the filling, while I squash the slices of bread together between my palms until they turn doughy and ooze peanut butter and jam goo, then gulp it down.

Sometimes we take tea like the Afs do, dunking our sandwiches into our green enamel mugs, then taking a dripping bite, followed by a swig, which we swill around in our mouths before swallowing. We have to pretend our sandwiches are nothing like the dainty little crustless quarters we're served, but are instead hunking Af door-stoppers. Anyway, it's called mixing cement and we aren't allowed to mix cement. If we get caught – spluttering cement and giggling – Mum hollers at us not to be so disgusting all our disgusting little lives. We only do it to sort of charf like Afs and in the end we always go back to the peeling-and-licking and mashing. Afterwards we loll around lizardly on the rough stone, licking crumbs off our fingers.

Cia is smaller than me, but not by much, and she's been here as far back as either of us can remember, but we've found that somehow, being bigger and older, I know all the things that Cia does not so I am the *induna*.

'What shall we do now?' she asks, after a while.

'Don' know,' is my reply. So we saunter on down to the swings – just worn tyres sawn in half and hung from a branch of an old acacia tree if I'm being truthful – in which we coil ourselves up, twisting the rope tighter and tighter until it will twist no more, then kicking off with our feet and spinning wildly undone. I feel a little ill but, still, it's a good way to pass the time.

Not for Cia, though. She's rocking dolefully now, waiting for something, anything, to disrupt the steady rhythm of our day. Over the years that have passed – seven and a half for Cia, eight and three-quarters for me – our days on the farm where we were both born have come to have a sameness about them, a metronome of ritual metring out the well-worn path of the sun across the faded blue sky.

And there's nowhere but the farm. It's far to the end of it – to the fence line that takes the fence boy days on end to get around – and far from there to anywhere. Dad says it's only twenty miles down the dirt road to Umtali, but twenty miles sure feels far when you're hanging on the back of the Landie.

Normally, after swinging, we plop ants into the ant-lion lairs under the swing tree. Ant-lion lairs are tiny ant-lion-made craters in the earth. Ants who slip (or get pitched) into a crater never get out – the sides are way too steep and too loose to climb – but the ants bust a gut trying, and that's what springs the trap: the dirt avalanche they set off, scrabbling frantically up the embankment, rouses the slumbering ant-lion. He claws his way out from a secret chamber beneath the lair and eats them alive.

But today is different. Today Cia gets just what she's been waiting for: an ear-splitting shriek pierces the air. We elbow out of our tyres and race down to the Afs' *khaya* towards the shrieking.

We arrive to find a chicken slaughter under way. Even though as many chickens hatch on the farm as are slaughtered, still Cia and I relish the slaughters. We clamber up the sides of the compost heap to get a bird's eye view from a warm nest of rotting vegetation churning with fat green chipolata worms.

We aren't really allowed to skulk around down by the *khaya* like two mongrels, but we go on down there and have us a good look. The compound buildings are low and squat with dark doorways yawning in the whitewash. All the farm workers live there, with their wives and *picanins,* about forty families. The compound is ringed by rickety mud huts with roofs made of bits of stick and hay, like in the three little pigs, and there are hordes of *picanins* scrambling about in the dirt courtyard that's been pounded and brushed bald. They are named Sipho, Themba, Javu and whatnot; they have scabby knees and belly-buttons that stick out like shiny black marbles. They stare at me and Cia something rude, but old Blessing's always nice to us. She squats down by the fire

5

and gives us a hunk of *sadza* dipped in sugar to suck. Our grandfather, Oupa, says we're naught better than a pack of scavengers.

The chickens that are going to die today have already been caught from the chicken run and brought to the executioner's block, the stump of an old tree – decently out of the other chickens' sight. They huddle together in their cage, clucking quietly, but to me it sounds quietly hysterical. The executioner, who is also our old houseboy Jobe, is standing by, an axe clasped in his hand, ready to behead the condemned chickens. Blessing, Jobe's wife, is busy plucking dead chickens at a galvanized sink a short way off, the water bloody and roiling with feathers. And while the whole business of the beheading makes for a great spectacle, it is really for the aftermath of a killing that we watch and wait. We sing the chorus from 'Here Comes the Axeman to Chop Off Your Head' in the interval.

'Chip, chop! Chip, chop! The last man's dead,' Cia yells lustily.

Then, pinioning a chicken by the neck, Jobe swings his axe. He slows for a heartbeat at the height of his arc. There is a sharp intake of breath from Cia, and she grips my wrist as the blade falls, severing the chicken's head. We flinch. And then, incredibly, headless and lifeless, the chicken wrenches free and proceeds to run in wild circles, blood spurting from the gaping artery. Cia's nails dig deeper and deeper into my flesh as the chicken performs its dance of death, until at last, drained of its lifeblood and spirit, it falls. Only when it lies utterly still does she let go, leaving behind small white crescents in my skin. I hear a warm, damp sigh close to my ear. Over and over we watch, stricken, as a chicken, dead but still alive, dances for us.

It is late afternoon by the time we head wearily back along the winding track towards the farmhouse, our shadows grotesque by the time it comes into view. I am shadowed, too, by foreboding.

The old house feels like a ruin, somehow. The pillars stationed along the length of the front veranda are being slowly strangled by Zimbabwe creeper, and a frilly grey lichen is feeding off the gangrenous roof slate. Inside, the house is high-ceilinged, cool and dark, but the 'art deco' tiles, imported from Europe for the entrance hall, are fractured now, crisscrossed with dark veins, and the Zambezi teak beams in the rest of the house are rotten in places. They creak and groan in the night as if tortured in their sleep by something that prowls up there in the eaves.

Its name is Modjadji, the rain goddess, and it was built by our great-grandfather in 1912, which is so long ago that there is no one still alive who remembers it. The year is carved in relief on an oval white plaque set into the plaster of the Cape Dutch gable. Sometimes I think of the hands that carved it in 1912, dead hands. It was Great-grandfather who first staked the surrounding land in the shadow of the Vumba mountains, which are in the east of our country, Rhodesia. Oupa tells over and over the tale of how Great-grandfather had to toil for years to hew the farm from the savage African land. It was his blood, sweat and tears that watered the earth, and every generation since has borne his legacy. It is Cia's and my duty to bear Great-grandfather's legacy too, when the time comes, although it is a crying shame we aren't sons.

There is a faded sepia daguerreotype of Great-grandfather, framed in ornate pewter, standing on the mantel above the stone hearth in the *voorkamer*. Sometimes I hoist Cia up so she can snatch it down, and we pore over it, somehow yoked to this echo of the past. To be honest, though, in his old-fashioned collar, with his stiffness and haughty chin, Great-grandfather looks rather forbidding. It's in his eyes most of all – they're colourless and polite. After a while, I have to turn away. If I look at that portrait for too long, I can feel his ghostly eyes *watching*.

Outside, the decay goes on, but it is a glorious kind of decay. Decadent. The air is sultry, perfumed, but with a sweetly sick scent – 'putrid', Oupa says. It seems to soften the light, veiling the too-vivid colours in the garden. 'Bloody obscene,' he says of it, shaking his head. 'Like a Parisian bordello.'

Bougainvillaea spills down from a tall conifer, huge tree ferns unfurl themselves from the time before Eden, and the soil in which Cia and I love to root is rich and loamy and slithers with dark, slimy creatures of the underworld. Ripe mangoes burst, their fermenting guts gorged on by fat fruit-flies who die drunk, bloated and addled in the sun.

'It's what happens when you try to foist England on savagery,' Oupa mutters darkly. 'Gets all corrupted like – rank and fetid. But will that mam of yours, nostalgic for something she's never known, ever see past her quaint, too-garish flowerbeds to the stink of corruption underneath? Will she buggery!'

He broods for a while. 'What is it she won't see, lasses?'

'The stink of corruption, Oupa.'

'Aye, that she won't, quixotic as she is wont to be. Her and her fancies.'

Mom ignores Oupa and the stink, though. She may have given up on Modjadji – the great rotting hulk – but to her garden she is devoted.

The terraces carved up the steep mountainside behind the house grow ever more unruly as they climb higher, until they disappear into the dark tangle of virgin forest.

Tree pythons slowly tighten their hold on the boughs of their host trees, their long, serpentine roots grasping back down to the soil; the lush undergrowth is alive with the whisper and clawing of small, secret lives; fungus sprouts from slick, rotted tree trunks, suckling on death.

In the forest, the living prey upon the dead.

There are ancient Shangani warriors buried up there, and sometimes the rains plunder the graves, washing the warrior skeletons down the mountain, angering the ancestors, cursing the earth.

Oupa calls it Paradise Lost, and it's Cia's and mine.

Today, though, homeward bound, my unease has solely to do with the matter of us wearing our ponchos. They are magnificent, crocheted in every shade of ice-cream imaginable and fringed with tassels, but splattered now with chicken blood and smeared with compost heap. This morning when I pulled them off their coat-hangers at the back of our

9

wardrobe it had seemed a fine idea. Even Cia didn't take much persuading.

'*Jislaaik*, man, Nyree!' She sucked in her breath and flicked her wrist. 'You're gonna get it!'

'Why? Are you gonna tell, *hey*?' I spat, as scornfully as I could.

She stared at me for a long, loaded moment, then at the ponchos, and succumbed to the goading right there and then, telling me to shut up and snatching hers from my hand.

We each donned a poncho, then vigorously rubbed Vaseline jelly on to our cheeks to shine them up, and took turns shoving each other out of the way the better to see ourselves in the old stained mirror that's mounted on the door of our big wooden wardrobe. At the time, in her ice-cream poncho, with ridiculously shiny cheeks, Cia was most pleased with herself, but she sure is sorry now. Matters are made worse because she is wearing my purple leotard underneath her blood- and slime-streaked poncho. Secretly, I'm scared witless of Mom catching us, and catch us she surely will.

As I glance up, I spy her lying in wait for us on the *stoep*, she having spotted the ponchos from some way off. I shove my hands deep into my dungarees pockets and whistle tunelessly, as if I haven't a care in this world, while out of the corner of my eye I see Cia trying for a bashful-like smile, but she ends up looking sassy.

Cia's face has a cheekiness about it that cheats her of her sweetness, and a smile like a Cheshire cat that slits her eyes. All up, she reminds you of a small, wickedly smug Chinese monkey – but cute in a way against which I can't compete. Still, cute won't save either of us today. As we reach the steps, my whistling gets more tuneless, while Cia gives up and looks plain scared.

I don't blame her. Mom has a face on her enough to scare the bejesus out of anyone. She stares and says not a word, which makes me start gabbling on about how me and Cia got attacked by a *khaya* dog that looked fit to have rabies, and how he tried to eat the ponchos and how we were lucky to escape being eaten ourselves, but Oupa, from the shadows behind Mom, says he can see the lie festering in my teeth, and Mom, without even deigning to bring up the beastly business of the ruined ponchos, just hisses, 'Get to your room. Now. And come out for supper only if you want to be thrashed to within an inch of your lives.'

I trudge upstairs with Cia on my tail. We're supposed to sit and think about how ashamed we are of ourselves, but later on, hungry and bored instead of ashamed, we spy on the Man instead. Every night after the generator dies, we take up our sentry posts. Kneeling on my bed, draped in the secret shadowy space beneath the bottle-green Paisley swirls of the curtains, Cia clutching Grover, her mangy, one-eyed teddy bear, we watch him through the pane. Lurking in the shadows of the neighbouring shed, he seems to be wearing a trilby tilted over his face and a long, shapeless trenchcoat. He stands utterly still, threatening. Part of me knows he isn't really there, that he's just shadows and light, but I still watch him with something crawling up the nape of my neck.

Afterwards I lie in the dark, my heart pounding from my

chest cavity into my head, listening to its echo through my pillow. It sounds uncannily like the crunching of footsteps on gravel.

'Nyree?' Cia whispers, in the spidery darkness. 'Are you awake?'

Silence.

'*Nyreee*,' she whispers again, insistently.

I pretend to mumble sleepily.

'Can I come and sleep in your bed? *Pleease?*'

I sigh. '*All right*, then,' I say in a tone I don't feel, but which I know both of us need to hear. Cia and Grover scramble across the spidery, crawling corridor between our beds and we snuggle down gratefully together.

2

'Dereliction of duty,' drones Oupa, 'is the very road to perdition.'

As familiar as Cia and I are with Oupa's sermons – since it is plain that part of *our* duty is to listen to them every day – we often don't understand the words, which sound like words from the Holy Bible. But of the gist we are in no doubt: duty and damnation. Duty, and getting damned for not doing it, is always the crux of Oupa's sermons, and enthroned on the *stoep* in his old cane armchair, which fans out regally behind him, swilling gin and tonic, he sure can deliver them.

Most days they are about Great-grandfather's toiling (although Cia and I, having discussed this in private, suspect that it was probably more like Great-grandfather supervising the Afs toiling).

Mom sits in the library at the big desk inlaid with leather on which Cia gouged her name, doing the accounts for the farm, scribbling columns of tiny numbers in marbled ledgers, a crease between her brows. We're not allowed to barge in or make a racket or, so help her, God, we'll get a flogging. We see her dark head bent over – she pulls her hair back into a ponytail. Oupa's supposed to be helping me with my homework, but he'll be buggered if he's going to play governess now on top of nanny and I can chant the six times table to myself when I'm on the bog. We sit and hear about the toiling instead.

Some days Jobe comes and rescues us. He leaves Philemon, his helper, to do the pile of ironing and carts us off in Washington the garden boy's wheelbarrow to make mud men without Oupa so much as noticing. Once in a while, Oupa strays off the virtues of toiling. It's usually a day on which someone died long ago, a day of heavier-handed gins and flushed, wobbling jowls. On flushed-jowl days we get to hear about Great-uncle Seamus instead.

Great-uncle Seamus, Oupa's dead brother, is a good deal more interesting than endlessly toiling Great-grandfather. It would seem that not everyone in this family has borne their duty as well as they ought. Great-uncle Seamus for one went 'astray'.

Despite our wiliest attempts to coax Oupa, we are still rather vague on what 'going astray' entails, but from the cursing of his brother's memory we reckon it must be wicked indeed. What he's divulged so far is that Great-uncle Seamus was a Prodigal Son and a Scoundrel who ran away from his duty on the farm, lived a debauched life in the city, where he did hell-raising, shovelled shame and disgrace upon the O'Callohan family name, and is now dead and buried – not in the family graveyard on the farm but in the cemetery in town. Cia and I once saw his tombstone, on which is carved 'Here lies Seamus O'Callohan – shot in a skirmish with a kaffir ', shocking and thrilling at the same time.

Today I reckon we're definitely headed for flushed jowls, and I can see Cia is already straining to hear more scandalous details with which to garnish Great-uncle Seamus. She is not disappointed.

'Where does it lead, lasses? The dereliction of duty?'

'Straight to perdition, Oupa.'

'Aye, that it surely does.'

And why? Because of Sloth. There are those – wastrels and other classes of reprobate – who fail miserably in their duty and all because of wanton idleness. Seamus, Oupa is sorry to say, was undoubtedly just such a wastrel who was afflicted with a general slovenliness of character.

He shakes his head. 'And it were a taste of forbidden fruit what were his final downfall too.'

Oupa wears both Africa and his European ancestors on his old face. It's a strong face, stubborn in its jutting jaw, creased like that of an old leatherback turtle, and he's bald but for a great twirling moustache, about which he's mightily conceited. Even though Oupa is seventy years old, it doesn't stop him bragging about his brawn, his cast-iron constitution and whatnot. At the same time, though, he has a high fore-head, a nose like the Romans in *Asterix and Obelix*, flinty blue eyes, one made of glass – and something that reminds me of the sepia ghost of his cold, polite father. Grisly yet noble, he has a ferocious temper, and when he is in a dark mood we are deeply in awe of him. So, though we're dying to hear more about Seamus's forbidden fruit, we daren't interrupt to ask. We let him be to brood for a while until he goes on in his own good time.

'And me brother mouldering in his grave these long years, it's not right his spawn should awaken the dead now. No good comes from sins of the flesh, lasses, no good. That is why they have an especially hot place in hell for adulterers.'

Getting damned by Oupa for sinning is not as bad as it sounds. In truth he is a heretic, Mom says, as wont to blaspheme as preach. Many times Cia and I have stood witness by him on the *stoep*, shotgun in hand, loudly threatening to set the Foul Minions of Satan upon the Bible-thumping heads of the Jehovah's Witnesses who from time to time trespass on his property. I wonder if me and Cia are the Foul Minions and what we'll do if we're set upon them.

Oupa got excommunicated years ago and says he is proud to have been an unrepentant heathen ever since. On account of his lost immortal soul, a delegation of Afrikaans sales ladies from the Dutch Reformed Church regularly descends on him, budding beards on their wobbling chins, to bring him God's word, lemonade and *soet koekies*. At the end of the meeting, they hug their Bibles sniffily to their bosoms, then squeeze his knee and gloat, and reassure Oupa that they are praying for him.

Nevertheless, sinners or not, I'd like to know more about who has woken the dead and am just trying to work out how to steer Oupa back to the business of the spawn when he spots a vervet tail dangling from the branch of a nearby acacia.

16

'Quick, lass, get me catty from me bedside drawer! I'll get that insolent vermin if it's the last thing I do!'

Oupa hates vervet monkeys' guts. His chief foe is the troop that live in the grove of acacia trees just outside the back door and constantly send raiding parties into the kitchen to whip whatever they can, the thieving bastards. When we were little, we used to believe Oupa's vervet-monkey lies. The lies were about how we'd been born monkeys ourselves, but how we'd been caught when we were still babies, skinned and detailed and our tails hung in a tree for *biltong*. Oupa reckons that when we got here, the *munts* were still swinging from the trees too. I wonder what happened to their tails. Then one day Cia confided to me that her tail was growing back. I inspected her rump and saw that, sure enough, she was sprouting a new stump. Neither of us was surprised. We figured that soon she'd grow fur and whatnot and turn back into a vervet monkey. Cia told me she would have to go and live with the other monkeys in the acacia trees. I was jealous and a bit tearful, but Cia looked right pleased with herself.

The vervets know that Oupa is their enemy and the last line of defence between them and our food, and their battles are epic. Oupa stations himself under the canopy of matted grapevines that shade the *stoep* by the kitchen, carefully conceals his weapon and, with infinite patience, pretends to doze off in his cane chair. It's called a ruse, and them vervets are either really stupid or else they're too greedy for their own good because they fall for it every time. If they had any brains they'd hold off, but the temptation is too much for them, and they make stealthily for the kitchen door the instant Oupa's head falls on to his chest.

As the first monkey swings down from the lowest branch of the closest acacia and furtively wraps his little fingers around the lintel, Oupa uncoils like a viper, aims and fires his catty at the prowler, who shrieks hysterically, whether he's taken a hit or not, inciting panic and a tree-canopy equivalent of a plains stampede. As soon as they've retreated a safe distance, the monkeys howl their outrage, shake the branches and bombard Oupa with all manner of missiles. Like some wily old fox, Oupa sits in the din, pods and twigs raining down on him, his thumbs hooked through his braces, a satisfied smile on his lips.

Best of all, though, is when Oupa dozes off for real in the late afternoon, muttering on to his chest, and we desert our post. We creep to the back of the *stoep*, which runs the whole way around the house, climb through a secret hole in the Terr fence and flee into the forest.

The forest is a shadowy otherworld of whispering and secrets. Actually, Cia and I possess the uncommon power to live in two worlds at once – the world you can see, and the other, the one you can feel. It's always there, all around us, beating its feathery wings just below. Cia can sense it, but I am the clairvoyant, and while she sees through my second sight, always it is the forest that opens my eyes.

Sometimes we catch other glimpses – at night fairies can easily be mistaken for glow-worms glowing faintly under bushes, and once, while burying my favourite food in the back garden by the light of the full moon – a fail-safe remedy for warts – I saw an explosion of fairies in the night sky (Oupa said they'd set off SOS flares at the next-door farm). Cia saw the Wombles climbing up our drainpipe one night, but the sighting had a nightmarish quality: apparently they were Wombles-Gone-Bad, who were coming to get her.

Other glimpses come to us from other eyes. When Dad was a boy, he woke once in the middle of the night to find all his toys had come alive, and though I've wished on everything I can think of and prayed to Jesus with all my might, I still haven't caught mine alive yet. Cia may be jinxing it, though: she lives in terror of the same thing – her beloved toys bewitched – and squeezes her eyes shut at the slightest stir in our bedroom at night.

But though we live in a world laced with threads of magic, triflings like tooth mice and firefly fairies pale next to the powerful magic that dwells in the forest. When Cia and I enter its unending twilight, the earthly gives way to the unearthly, to the ethereal. As the canopy of trees closes over us we can hear the heavy boughs whispering ancient secrets to one another, just as they do in the tales of the Faraway Tree, and we can feel hidden eyes on us with every footfall. Shrouded in the forest, we are lifted above the grubbiness of chicken slaughters, of peanut butter and jam, and are allowed to enter another world – one where things flit on gossamer wings and anything is a mere wish away.

We have a hideout, just like the Secret Seven, except ours is better. On one of the old terraces above the farmhouse a curtain of ivy trailing down from a stinkwood opens on to an alcove ringed with stones from the ruins of the old terrace buttress. It is on the edge of the forest and where we will go tonight for the flight to Fairyland.

For months Cia has been begging me to take her with me. At first I said no and told her it was because she was too fat for the delicate wings that I sprout each night at midnight, and that that great gut of hers would probably sink us both, but Cia went right on begging, and after a while her begging wore me down. And now darkness has fallen on the night that I have promised to take her.

We wait for a long time after the light has gone off under Mom's door, waiting for her to get drowsy, for sleep to come. We nearly fall asleep ourselves – I keep jerking awake on the floor against the door to our room. At last I judge it safe and we open our door, the latch creaking disloyally, and creep out into the passage. It is cloaked in velvety darkness, but we know its long, wide expanse and the doorways opening off it. Mom and Dad's is at the far end, the empty room next to it, the bathroom is opposite and our room last. We make it safely to the landing, not having to pass Mom's door, and slink down the spiral staircase, but as we reach the bottom and head out into the entrance hall past the *voorkamer* and towards the great front doors, we suddenly hear Oupa call out from the back bedroom: 'Who's there?'

I freeze. Cia's nails dig deep into the delicate skin of my wrist and I try to stifle my breathing.

'*Jislaaik!* We'll be in trouble if we get caught,' Cia warned, before nightfall. What with the Terrs and hyena, we are never allowed to wander beyond the Terr fence after dark.

We clutch each other in the hallway, waiting for the strip

20

of light to appear under Oupa's door, but it does not. He must have thought the night and sleep had deceived him. After an age I nudge Cia forward. We make it to the front door, and I wish again that there were another way out, such as climbing through our window and down a tree, like the Hardy Boys, but our window is barred and there's no escape. I unlatch the sash window that flanks the door and slowly crank it up. We slither out through the chink, first me, then Cia, tiptoe round to the back of the *stoep*, flee across the lawn like two nightgowned wraiths and climb through a secret hole in the Terr fence.

As we enter the forest, fear caresses me. Everything seems somehow transformed: shapes have shifted, there are strange sounds, and I feel an invisible presence that has never been here before. This is not how I imagined it would be. It is far more frightening out here alone in the darkness, and I have to summon every ounce of courage I possess to plunge into the depths of the forest. Only Cia's scared face, which looks up trustingly into mine, makes me muster the strength and, her hand clasped in mine, we go on.

On reaching the hideout, we warily lift the veil of ivy (lest we disturb some unknown nocturnal intruder) and crawl in. Cosseted inside our den, my fear begins to fade. The evil shadows ebb to hover just outside the threshold, while the night and the forest begin to cast a different spell. The hour is nigh and my excitement mounts. I compose myself, pull the chopstick wand from the elastic of my *broekies* and instruct Cia to prepare for the incantation to invoke the spirits.

We've learned it from spying on the Afs' ancestral ceremonies, and while we are vague on the details, many hours of rehearsal means we can do a passable imitation of such a ceremony. I assume the role of chief *n'anga* chanting an invocation that is part African shaman, part recital from our book by the Brothers Grimm, while Cia plays the supporting cast, ululating, swaying and beating on an imaginary drum.

'*Bayede Nkosi!*'

'Boom ba-ba boom ba-ba boom!'

Cia closes her eyes.

'Abracadabra!' I wave my wand and pray to the spirit of Angélique for divine intervention. Angélique is our dead grandmother, Oupa's wife, God rest her soul, and I'm named after her, or at least second-named after her, so I figure she's our best ancestor to pray to. Besides, I'm afraid to call upon Great-grandfather, toiling and toiling with his soulless eyes. Angélique is very mysterious too. Her secrets are locked away in the attic.

'Amen,' I say in ending. 'Peace be with you.'

Cia makes the sign of the cross.

'*Idlozi liyabekwela*,' I add, which means 'an ancestral spirit is watched for'.

Then I lie down solemnly on my stomach on a large granite block, Cia clambers on to my back, wraps her arms tightly round my middle, and we wait expectantly for my wings to grow.

Suddenly it is utterly still, with not even the ear-piercing shriek of a fruit bat to break the silence. We wait.

'Nyree?'

'*Ssssh!*'

The silence yawns.

'Nyree, why's nothing happening?' she whispers breathily into my ear.

'I don't know,' I hiss back irritably. 'It's probably because you're too heavy.'

'Oh.'

It is a single note of sheer disappointment.

I feel bad – for not taking Cia to Fairyland and, worse, for blaming her for my failure to do so. She clambers off my back and we sit glumly on the rock.

'I *knew* it. I just *knew* I'd never get there in the end,' she declares eventually, hanging her head.

'Yes, you will,' I say reassuringly. 'You know, I haven't been going that long, and maybe my wings will get stronger and I'll be able to take you after a while.'

'Do you think so?' Her face is hopeful.

'Yes, I'm *sure* I will,' I say, more convincingly now. 'In fact, maybe you'll even grow your own wings. I'll ask for you. I'll ask the Queen as soon as I go again. It might take a long, long time, but I'm sure she'll grant me a wish.'

Cia accepts this gratefully and, putting the whole sorry business behind us, we set off into the forest once more. But I can feel eyes following us back through the night and I know they are the eyes of the *amadlozi*. Hosts of them hover in the shadows: soulless-eyed Great-grandfather, Angélique with her secrets, Seamus of the sins of the flesh, and more gather behind them – watchful, hungry, patient.

3

Cia and I are foraging in Mom's vegetable patch. It's late afternoon and we've already covered most of the best ground. We are now in the pea rows, zigzagging methodically up and down, picking and popping shells and shovelling the peas into our mouths. Before the vegetable patch, we harvested the gooseberry bush under the back hedge, the granadilla by the kitchen window, and gorged ourselves a bruised purple on the mulberry trees out by the orchard. Over the years, we've got better than locusts at scavenging, and it is only once the very last vine in the very last row has been minutely and expertly inspected for pea pods of just the right plumpness that we trudge home, gloriously stained and satiated.

As we round the corner of the Afs' *khaya*, however, we lurch out of our languor: a great hulking beast pounces on us from the shadows. Cia yelps with delight. The beast is our dad, home from the bush, and he's been ambushing us this way for as long as we've been scavengers.

He's hairy, wearing camouflage and stinks – a mixture of sweat, smoke and gunmetal oil. With a coarse mesh draped over his curly head, he's even more beastly. As if I'm a bag of Willards crisps, he swings me up in the air and plants a kiss on my forehead. Then he hoists Cia on to his wide shoulders and the three of us set off, homeward bound, rowdily singing, 'We are the *shumba* drinkers, we drink a dozen a day.'

Dad is a hero and a stranger. He goes away for long, long stretches of time – we hardly notice he's gone, so used are we to his not being there – because he has to fight the Terrs. I've never seen a Terr, although when Cia asked me once, a long time ago, I told her how she could spot one: from his spoor, I reckon a Terr is about eight feet tall, he slobbers and his toenails are long, ragged and filthy. He tears the limbs off live vervet monkeys to gnaw and if he gets his hands on a cane rat, he guts it with a snaggletooth, then licks the entrails off his dripping chin. That's why his teeth are dark and rotted: if you feed on live animals, the blood stains them for ever. Cia nodded, satisfied, as if I'd confirmed what she'd suspected all along. But actually I know that Terr is short for 'terrorist' and Dad's always been fighting them because there's always been the War.

It is when Dad turns up that we notice. He descends on us like a long lost crusader, throwing the household into uproar. We love the *wildebees* stampede he sets off as he stomps around the farm marshalling the labourers, who've evidently grown slovenly in his absence. We trail after him as he wrestles pumps down by the deep algae- and leech-infested reservoirs, then wrestles herds of *mombies* through great troughs of pea-soup tick dip, and keeps on wrestling until the farm is restored to order. The wrestling is accompanied by a great deal of cursing, guttural grunts and haranguing of the slovenly troops.

'Hey, *eiwe*! What the hell've you *munts* been doing while I was away?' is how he interrogates Jobe.

He doesn't interrogate Mom, though. What the hell does he think she was doing while he was away? She wasn't doing anything slovenly, I can tell you, but still somehow things seem to have got themselves into a sorry state.

'*Eish*, Baas,' is Jobe's standard response.

In fact, Jobe's whole pretence at respect for the *baas* isn't very convincing. It's not disrespect exactly, it's just that he never knows what the hell the *munts*'ve been doing. He's not very sorry and sort of thinks the whole thing is funny. Dad barely seems to notice as he sucks and spits petrol from a blocked tank and spews a stream of perfunctory slurs in between.

Better still when Dad's home are the outings to the Umtali Farmers' Co-op on Saturday mornings. It is a vast warehouse down by the railway station in Umtali. It takes ages to get there – we have to hang on to the back of the Landie on the drive past the farms and the TTL.

The Tribal Trust Lands are where the Afs have their farms. They also have their own school there so they won't be sauntering into ours any time, and they don't come to our bi-scope in town, although I don't know where theirs is. They have their own special gate in the Terr fence around the farmhouse, except for Jobe who's always sneaking a shortcut through ours, even though Oupa tells him we get Important Visitors, and does Jobe think that the Important Visitors want to see a bunch of *munts* strutting up and down? The TTL we drive past on the way to Umtali is called Mutambara.

The revving of the Landie's engine stirs life in the small *kraals* that hug its rutted track; half-naked squealing children and scrawny dogs dash out behind the rear wheels, while wary older eyes watch from darkened doorways. There are chickens and tethered goats scratching in the stalks of the *mielie* patches, women carrying teetering buckets of water on their heads, babies strapped to their backs under brightly coloured blankets, and wonky hand-made Coca-Cola and Lux Soap signs on the *spaza* shops.

At the Farmers' Co-op, Cia and I get lost somewhere in the maze of chick, duckling and piglet pens, and after we're found in the lost-property office and hauled out to the car, we proceed to drip ice-cream from our 99s on to the seat until Cia throws up from the mechanical horse ride, and we're both banned from setting foot again within a hundred-mile radius of town, as God is Dad's witness.

Mom changes around him too. From striding around the farm in a pair of flared hipster denims, a rifle slung over one shoulder, not taking any nonsense from the likes of us, she lets her hair down, slips into satin petticoats and perfume and the timbre of her laughter changes. The world tilts dangerously, and I feel a little giddy.

When he's home, I remember the mother she was – a shyer, gentler mother. She used to wear shimmery green eyeshadow and make delicate little violet petals out of icing and she'd put '*Ipi Ntombi*' on the record-player and dance with us round the *voorkamer*, spinning faster and faster till we were all dizzy. Now she doesn't have time for that sort of malarkey. Now she wipes the sweat off her brow with the rolled-up sleeve of one of Dad's shirts. Oupa says it's wearing the war-widow mantle that crushes what's fragile in a young woman. I don't know about that. Dad's not dead, and whatever mantle the Mom I know wears, she's not wearing it when he returns, and the shadow of her past life can't be so fragile as it's still there underneath.

Whenever Dad's home, he and Mom stay up late into the night, on the *stoep* in summer and in front of the fire in winter, discussing the War. Sometimes Cia and I wrap ourselves around the banister to listen, more so now since we can tell that things are worsening.

Worse in what way we don't know, but Mom and Dad shake their heads and Dad whistles low and says things like, 'Christ, Amy, I don't know, I just don't know.' Lately they talk a lot about something bad that has happened in South Africa. South Africa is next door. It's criss-crossed by huge glittering highways that lead to the sea and also to a city called Johannesburg where there is gold and whole aisles in the giant supermarkets groaning with the kinds of sweets that sure make our sanction rations of niggerballs, gobstoppers and chocolate Fredo Frogs look measly by comparison.

The South Africans were our friends, but not any more, because they've done something bad. Me and Cia don't know what crime they committed, but it can't be good if all

29

the other nations have accused them of it. Seems they looked even guiltier by keeping up a friendliness with us, so now they've ended it, and Dad reckons that without another drop of fuel or a bullet, we're doomed. And we know what doomed means all right.

Oupa knew he could never trust the treacherous bastards anyway. The South Africans. Their time will come, though.

'White Africa is small and its borders are shrinking by the day, and here we are standing on the last bastion ready to fight to the death, which is more than you can say for the spineless, gutless Dutchmen who pawned us like Judas Iscariot. The miserable ingrates. But, oh, yes, they will pay the price of their perfidy. Their time will come.'

Why we need the bullets is because of the Terrs. There are hundreds of Terrs, different kinds too, and we need bullets for all of them. Some of the Terrs are Ndebele, who are a tribe from the south. Jobe is an Ndebele from Matabeleland. Dad swears and calls them the Bloody Ndebele. The leader of the Ndebele Terrs is a gorilla called Joshua Nkomo, although when me and Cia saw Joshua Nkomo on TV, it turned out he wasn't a gorilla at all, just a regular Af.

And now we are alone. No one will help us.

We can tell things are getting worse in other ways too. Oupa's taken to sitting on the *stoep* at sunset yelling '*Pamberi chongwe!*'

'*Pamberi chongwe*' is the Terrs' war cry. It means 'Forward the cock'. In the kitchen Jobe sucks his teeth, says, '*Eish,*' and shakes his head. Sometimes Mom rides past on her way back to the stables and just rolls her eyes. Then Oupa starts whooping and ululating, which sets off the dogs' howling, and Cia and I have to line up on the lawn and sing the chorus to 'We'll Fight for Rhodesia, Rhodesians Never Die!'.

So we're worried. The only other country we know of is England and they hate us because of the UDI, which was when Rhodesia got rid of the Queen, and every year Mom and Dad go to the Independence Ball to celebrate it.

We all drive down to Salisbury, through its avenues of purple velvet jacaranda trees, and stay at the Monomotapa Hotel, which is marvellous. A boy from our school called Dell also stays at the Monomotapa. His gang, the Dogs of War, gob out of their window on to the pool deck, then quickly duck their heads in so they don't get bust by the pool-patrol Afs. But we know who they are. Me and Cia fight the Dogs of War over the ice machine in the corridor. On the night of the ball, Mom is transformed into Cinderella and we stare and feel strangely shy. On the Sunday we're allowed to join the adults for lunch in the formal dining room of the grandest hotel in town, Miekles. There is a carvery and stiff linen napkins fashioned into crowns that we aren't allowed to wear on our heads, and a waiter sporting a red velvet pillbox fez. So we know all about the glory of the UDI. But England hates us because of it, so they sure as hell won't help us now. In assembly at school I've started to pray extra hard for the troopies.

Dad's visits never seem to last long, so whenever he comes home it's kind of like going on holiday – everything's disrupted – and the holiday ends as soon as he leaves to rejoin his stick in the bush. I can feel it coming to an end as me and Cia sit there watching Dad shove his ratpack into his kit bag while he instructs us on the fine art of bivouac-making. Then he hoists his pack on to his shoulders and disappears again from our lives, the only trace of him appearing in crêpey blue airmail paper letters, in which he sketches, for our benefit, stick figures of himself in the bush, armed to the teeth, stalking the Terrs.

4

'*Sis*, man! It stinks.'

Dell's brought a dead rat to school. We're standing at the bottom of the field in a huddle – me and Cia and the Dogs of War are in the thick of it – staring down at the dead rat. It's lying in Dell's unrolled *Spiderman* comic book. He found it last week and gave it to his dog, but his dog didn't like them dead so he buried it. Then he dug it up – and how come it hadn't gone to heaven?

'Its fur's gone kind of mangy,' says Cia.

Dell reckons he could skin it anyway. He'd like to shoot a lion and skin it. He's going to one day. He's going to shoot a lion and a leopard. He'll bring the skin back for Cia if she likes. In fact, he'll bring back loads of skins and tusks and claws for Cia.

Cia is sulking because Dell wouldn't let her play branders with us on account of her being in KG2 and a girl, and now she doesn't have any wet-tennis-ball weals to sport.

'So do you reckon Spiderman's true?'

'*Ja*, I reckon he's true.'

'Well, what would he do to a Terr if he was true?'

It's Dell who wants to know. He tips the rat on to the ground, rolls up his tattered *Spiderman* comic book and shoves it back down his shirt. He didn't see why Spiderman shouldn't be true. He thought he'd try it anyway. He got himself a wall spider, but it wouldn't bite him. He figured a radioactive one would probably be better but he didn't know where you could find one of those.

'More like you're a big scaredy-cat who'd sooner gargle wasps than try to get a radioactive wall spider to bite you.'

It's Jeremiah who reckons Dell's a big scaredy-cat. Jeremiah is one of the Dogs of War and he's always sneering and jeering at Dell.

'I'm not a scaredy-cat,' says Dell, witheringly, 'and you're a big cry-baby anyhow.'

Only Damian Gilchrist stays out of it – he's squatting on his haunches against the fence, apart from everyone. I know Dell is afraid of him. We all are. He bunks school all the time, just swaggers on out of the gate at big break sometimes – and he smokes behind the bicycle sheds and says, 'fuck off,' like he's not even trying.

I practised it on Cia. 'Fuck off.'

She stared at me. I could hear it punching her in the gut, but it didn't come out the way Damian Gilchrist does it. Like a shrug. I've smoked too. One time me and Cia stole one of Oupa's cigarettes, even though it'll be straight to boarding-school for us if we ever get bust, and smuggled it into school. A gang of us crouched around it and took turns

34

sucking and puckering up so that the smoke didn't just belch out of your mouth, but blew out in a nice thin hosepipe to prove you'd inhaled it. I was good at it. Damian Gilchrist smokes alone. We never do that. Once Dell and me came round the bicycle sheds and saw Damian Gilchrist there smoking alone. We hunkered down next to him. We couldn't help it – just saw him and then, next thing we knew, we were squatting next to him. Damian Gilchrist exhaled. The smoke spewed out in a thin, perfect coil.

'Want a drag?' he said, offering the cigarette.

I couldn't believe it. I'd reckoned he was going to sneer at us. When it was my turn my hand shook, but no one said anything. It was a Camel, the cigarette. They're the toughest and the Camel guy in the advert at the bi-scope is the hardest. Much better than the Peter Stuyvesant people, who do nothing but go to Monte Carlo and lounge around and that. The Camel guy's all alone. He has to dive off his boat in the middle of the Amazon jungle and hack out the weeds caught in his propeller. Then he has a Camel. I took a small drag and passed the fag to Damian. It was disgusting. My stomach lurched and I started sweating. I thought I was going to honk right there. I swallowed the honk, and the smoke on top of it, and shuddered. Then I gasped and the smoke came out long and thin like it's supposed to. I'd done it.

'That was fucking lovely,' said Dell. 'I love smoking, don't you?'

Dell was talking too much. He knew it.

None of us has ever bunked. Dell reckons he's gonna, real soon. Once he said he had, but really he was just hiding in the boys' toilets because he hadn't done his maths home-work. One time Damian carved his name on the big tree down by the athletics track with his Swiss army knife that you aren't allowed to bring to school. Also, he sang rude words to the tune of 'Amazing Grace' in assembly, plus he has a pet bushbaby and he spat into the Coke fountain at the Umtali trade fair and he doesn't care if anyone saw him or not and he doesn't even tell anyone what he did.

Dell and the other boys try to get nearer him. Damian Gilchrist. They copy the way he stands. Slouches more like. He has no friends, though. He could have a gang of his own if he wanted, but he doesn't belong to any gang and he does-n't dare anyone either. He's gone further than that.

Then the bell goes and we have to go back to class. Miss Lovemore is my teacher, and Dell's and the Dogs of War's too. She's pretty and she smells nice, and at the end of the day she reads us stories from a big book called *O Best Beloved*, which happen on the banks of the great grey-green greasy Limpopo river all set about with fever trees. I don't think she likes us much, though. And she slaps you with a ruler if you get back late from break.

Just as we head off to class Dell turns to me and says, 'Hey, Nyree, my mom says you're getting yourselves an urchin or somethin'. I heard her talking to my dad about it.'

'What's an urchin?' I feel foolish having to ask him.

'Don' know, but the way she said it, it can't be good. She said something like, "Shame, poor Amy O'Callohan." And then she said that your mom's got loads on her plate, what with the farm and you and Cia running round like wild dogs,

36

and now she's gone and inherited some little urchin from a cousin too. Do you think it's like a dog?'

I wonder. A few days ago a battered old Datsun was parked outside the house when we came round the corner of the track that winds up the hill from the *khaya*. Cia got herself in a flurry over someone unknown coming to the farm.

'Come on, man – Nyree, run!' she shouted, looking all eager.

We raced up the track, but before we neared Modjadji, a lady sporting big dark glasses and a red boob-tube walked out of the front door followed by Mom and Oupa. She tripped down the steps, climbed back into the Datsun and spluttered away. Cia skidded to a halt, her arms windmilling.

'*Aaah!* Damn it!' she swore.

When we asked who she was, Oupa muttered about spawns of past sins, but Mom told us she was a cousin of our father's and she'll explain later and to look at the mud we'd dragged into her hallway. But I don't have time to wonder about the red boob-tube lady for long: Cia's got to get back under the fence of the KG playground.

After big break it's history. I'm slumped over my desk ignoring Dell, who is flicking an elastic band at the back of my head. Flies buzz drowsily against the window-panes. The history is about how the whites got to Africa. They came from Europe, which is where things were imported from before there were sanctions and why we are still called Europeans, even though neither Cia nor I has ever seen Europe. Anyway, they were poor and grimy and had to toil in factories and whatnot in the Industrial Revolution and it was easy to get them to come to Africa, with free passage and a promise of land on the eastern frontier of the Cape Colony.

Oupa reckons they were poor dumb bastards, most of whom couldn't tell the arse-end of a hoe from a Mauser, dispatched as unpaid soldiers of the realm to defend it against the barbarians clamouring at the gate.

After they got to Africa, they turned into pioneers. They crossed the Limpopo and then Chief Lobengula gave Matabeleland to Queen Victoria. In our history book there's a drawing of great blubbery Chief Lobengula squatting on the ground holding a beaded fly switch. Next to it is the treaty. I had a good look at the funny elephant stamped on a blob of red wax at the bottom of it. Then Lobengula went back on his word so the pioneers killed him. He died on the banks of the Shangani river, deserted by all but a few loyal *impi*, and in 1893 Rhodesia was started. Now on Rhodes and Founders Day we get the day off school.

I don't tell Miss Lovemore what Oupa said about the pioneers, though.

She looks at my homework and says, 'Very nice, Nyree.'

We had to colour in an ox-wagon. Mine's got an orange hood and red wheels. Dell didn't do his and Miss Lovemore doesn't even want to hear his excuse. I didn't do mine very neatly, though; some of the red crayon sticks out from the spokes. I did it in a hurry because I was trying to get away from Oupa who said he's doubtful about the guts and glory of standing squarely behind the barrel of an old Mauser massacring a horde of *impi* armed to the teeth with naught but sharpened mangoes.

After the last bell, we have to go to a special assembly. We line up outside the hall and the prefects prowl up and down the lines checking for who isn't wearing their blazer and hat. Dell hasn't pulled up his blackjack-spiked socks and he's going to find himself rapping on Mr McCleary's door if he carries on like that. Then we file in in silence. Mr McCleary stands behind the lectern with the Bible on it. He hawks and tells us in his most solemn voice about how the Terrs shot down an aeroplane called the Hunyani. They shot it down with a rocket that the Russians gave them specially. The captain radioed, 'Mayday! Mayday!' then crash-landed the plane because he was brave and valiant. Then Mr McCleary tells us to bow our heads while he says the special prayer for God to bless all the dead Hunyani people, especially the little kids who were innocent lambs.

After assembly I amble on down to the main gate to meet Jobe and Cia. Jobe comes to fetch us every day – he rides on one horse and brings another for us. Today he's come on Joe Soap and brought Fivel for us, Cia's favourite. Cia is already draped over Fivel's neck like a rag doll. Fivel wouldn't let anyone else drape themselves over him like that, but he loves Cia, so he stands there all docile and munches grass.

'Jobe, how come Dell's rat didn't go to heaven?' Cia asks worriedly, on the way home.

She must've been worrying about it ever since big break.

'He was dead and Dell buried him and then he dug him up and he hadn't gone to heaven.'

'Ah, now, that is because the *amadlozi* aren't needing rats in heaven, and because the *n'anga* needs the rat's claw to make a special *muti*. So when a snake or a scorpion bites you, you scratch the skin with the rat's claw to let out the blood and the poison will be gone.'

'What about Fivel? Will he go to heaven?'

'Oh, yes, Fivel. Fivel is going to go to heaven, *ingane*. There is no making *muti* out of Fivel.'

5

After Dad's departures, things go back to normal. While Mom manages the farm, Oupa does his bit by managing the Afs. This means roving about the farm, me and Cia roving behind him, instilling the fear of God Almighty in the workers.

Once Oupa's staked out a work site, which is to say, once he's selected a mock pulpit for himself, he summons the workers. They look none too pleased about being summoned, but having no say in the matter they stop working and shuffle on up to him. As soon as they've stopped shuffling, there's a deep growling in Oupa's chest, which growls on up out of his throat. That is the cue. The crowd falls silent. Cia and I stand rigid. Then Oupa raises his right hand and, before a dozen pairs of eyes, plucks out his own left eye from its socket. There's a gasp from the horrified onlookers and the lid puckers over the eyeless hollow. Then Oupa lays the eye reverently on a rock.

'This, my friends, is the Evil Eye, so it is,' he thunders. 'It

41

will lie here and watch over you for me, lest any of you be tempted to slack off on the job.' He hisses the last part about slacking off.

The Evil Eye is made of glass – bafflingly, he lost his old one in the deserts of Egypt to one of 'Rommel's Jerry henchmen' – and he must put it to work to curb slovenliness creeping in since we don't tolerate slackers on this farm. As we know the eye can't see, we're only half afraid of it so are totally scornful of the Afs' fear – although, given Dad's verdicts on the state of slovenliness whenever he returns home, fear is evidently a less effective ploy than Oupa imagines.

Effective or not, though, Oupa is forbidden to do it. He's been told to desist on numerous occasions by Mom, but is so far undeterred. Once he returned to find his eye smashed to smithereens. We weren't surprised. Every time Oupa performs the eye hex, a low, angry murmur surges through the assembled crowd. It was a matter of time before someone's resentment overcame their superstition and they destroyed the reviled eye. But not even that incident deterred Oupa. To Cia's and my delight, he wore an eye-patch fit for a pirate for a while, which he said made him look rakish, but as soon as his new eye arrived from South Africa, he pulled off the rakish, piratical patch and went back to sorcery.

Today Oupa is standing on top of a tractor-pulpit by the sheds. Me and Cia are crouched in our makeshift bivouac in its giant wheel, listening to him deliver an invigorating sermon on the Deadly Sin of Sloth. I'm starting to get pins and needles in my feet when Oupa, with a flourish, plucks the eye from its socket to a gratifying gasp from the crowd.

Then I hear, over the gasp, 'Patrick O'Callohan! What in God's name are you doing?' and look up to see Mom pushing her way to the front of the crowd. She's never caught Oupa in the act before – she's always had to rely on second-hand witness accounts. She launches into a sermon of her own, but Oupa just turns his one eye on her balefully and says a curse. Oupa pretends that Mom's not the boss when Dad's away. Mostly she lets him pretend, but we can tell he's gone too far this time.

'You simply cannot behave like this, Patrick. Not even your son would tolerate it,' she informs him grimly.

At dinner Mom tells me and Cia that we've got a cousin. Cia stops chewing. We've never had a cousin before. The cousin's mother is the daughter of Great-uncle Seamus.

'*Illegitimate* daughter,' Oupa adds, in a clipped tone.

She's asked us to care for her son for a while.

'Dumped her little bastard on us, more like.'

Mom purses her lips. 'For God's sake, Patrick, he is your own blood. It's only right that we take him in.'

After dinner Cia asks me what illegitimate is. I explain that it's the condition of being afflicted with illness, probably rotgut. I don't know what a little bastard is – the boob-tube lady didn't have anyone with her that could be the little bastard.

'Everything's the wrong way round,' Oupa laments on the *stoep* that evening, 'There's 'er with 'er bastard, and your own mam barren when it comes to a son and heir.' He shakes his head sorrowfully. 'Lasses will be the ruin of this whole family, you know,' he prophesies.

43

'Sorry, Oupa,' offers Cia, sounding genuinely penitent.

Oupa looks down at her, as though noticing for the first time her small presence crouched at his feet. His expression softens and the corner of his mouth even twitches. 'It's all right, lass,' he says indulgently, ruffling her already ruffled blonde tresses.

The cousin is a boy who is fourteen. Cia wants to know when we are going to see him. Mom says we can't because he's in boarding-school. I am shocked – boarding-school is a place with which we are regularly threatened by Dad when we've misbehaved. Dad had the misfortune himself of attending that God-forsaken hell-hole as a boy. Oupa, who attended it in his day, calls it a venerable old institution, but behind his back, Dad reckons it was a bloody torture chamber.

I don't know how come Oupa nods slowly and calls it the venerable old institution all solemn, like it's a great place. While Dad's never actually told me and Cia what sort of tor-turing went on, Oupa has. It was on the *stoep*, Oupa on his throne, tiny red veins sprawled across his jowls, when he told us about how his brother had run away from boarding-school. And not just the once either.

'He was a lad of scarcely five, Seamus, when they sent him there. I remember my father telling him to stop blub-bering like a bairn as he prised him from the bosom of our nanny. Then he shook his hand and left him in that alien place of long Gothic corridors that stank of soggy cabbage and wax polish where no one ever touches you.

'I knew he'd be all right, though. Seamus was the tough-est damn kid I ever met. He could catch snakes with his bare

44

hands, just stole up on them and pinched them at the nape of the neck, then held them up for me writhing like demons possessed. He had a squint left eye and wore a necklace of warthog tusks and he never cried, not ever, not when he got called names, or got spat on or even when he got stoned out of the marula tree at the bottom of the playground like a *kaffir* chicken.

'Anyway, Seamus was just about okay when we both got summoned to the headmaster's office to be told that our mam was dead. Seamus just stood there hanging his head, like he was in trouble. I wasn't even sure if he was listening. That night he ran away.

'Took them three days to catch him. They found him hitching his way home. Everyone reckoned he was deader than a *kaffir* dog caught with his curly tail in the chicken house and that'd teach him a lesson. They dragged him back and gave him a thrashing in front of the whole assembly. He deserved it, of course. He was only seven but he took it like he deserved it too, but he bolted again before his bruises had mottled yellow.'

Oupa shook his head slightly, then winced his eyes shut.

'Do you want to know the truth, though, lasses? The truth is I admired him. Part of me was rooting for that little bugger, hoping they wouldn't get him. Officially it was an embarrassment for me. By then I was higher up the ranks. I'd attained the giddy heights of prefect. I was saluted, I'd made it. A regular Tom Brown, I captained the cricket team, pelted new boys with marulas on their way back to the dorms from the grub hall, spelled tradition with a capital T. Me brother going AWOL every five minutes was at my cost. But secretly I envied him.'

Hearing that Oupa was a prefect left Cia and me deeply impressed. After Oupa's telling us about what happened to Seamus in boarding-school, though, we're worried about the bastard boy who got sent away there. But worrying doesn't help and we've got to listen to our Bible story.

It's Oupa's punishment for the eye hex. Mom told Oupa that we are being raised with the most warped notions about religion. Indeed, our religious instruction has thus far been found wanting. To remedy this, and with due consideration of his role in warping us, Oupa is henceforth to read Bible stories to us in the evenings. When he tried to protest, she merely silenced him with her hand. 'They deserve the choice, Patrick. And you're going to give it to them.'

Oupa scowled. It's a cheek if you ask me. I reckon that Mom doesn't even say her prayers. When me and Cia are late for bed and Cia's trying to think of ways to stay up even later, she tells Mom we haven't said our prayers yet, but Mom just says that doesn't matter, go and brush your teeth and get into your pyjamas this instant.

Oupa reckons he's under surveillance so there's nothing for it, we'll get our dose of the Good Book, although he can't be blamed for the taking of a few liberties here an' there, now, can he?

'And so, lasses, there stands Jesus on the mount, all the world below Him, Lucifer leering at His side,' says Oupa, the-atrically. '"All this could be yours for ever, if you'll just kneel down and worship me." He tries to tempt Jesus once more.

'But Jesus, though He be weak and hungry from his forty days and forty nights in the desert, rises up,' and Oupa's voice is quavering now, 'and He says unto the Prince of Darkness, *"Never, Satan! Never! Now get thee hence!"* And He punches the Devil right in the guts and hurls him off the mountain, and the Devil is smashed to a bloody pulp on the rocks below.'

'Good!' yells Cia, with gusto.

We only find out at school that there are other versions of these events. When the Wisdom of Solomon (which is this story about how King Solomon pulled some baby in half) is read out one day in assembly by a stuttering, red-faced boy, Cia, at its conclusion, shouts indignantly from the front row, 'That's not how it goes!' Then she sings 'Onward Christian Soldiers' so loudly that people in the front row turn around to stare.

Following the awkward phone call from our headmaster, who feels Cia's version to be inappropriate and frankly disturbing, our home religious education is aborted. Oupa looks almost disappointed.

Now that Oupa's banned from anything to do with religion, pagan or otherwise – or he'll be banished to the old-age home without so much as his false teeth – his contribution to the smooth running of the farm is confined to waging war on the ever-encroaching African wild. 'A formidable commission, lasses,' he informs us. 'As one of the last outposts of civilization, we are under constant siege by the savage hosts of Africa. Holding them at bay is without respite and requires a disposition of unusual tenacity, as well, I regret to tell you, as the grace to suffer ingratitude of the worst kind.' Oupa sighs self-pityingly. 'Why do we need the grace, lasses?'

'To suffer ingratitude of the worst kind, Oupa.'

Oupa nods sadly.

When he's not on vervet detail, Oupa mounts campaigns against the legions of invading invertebrates, from white ants who secretly eat the wood in the farmhouse leaving nothing but husks in their wake, to swarms of technicoloured locusts who simply devour everything, to the disease-carrying flesh-eaters.

'The steaming tropics of Africa have fomented the greatest proliferation of life on Earth, lasses. But there is a special kind of horror – a primeval horror – of life that has evolved exclusively to prey on human flesh,' Oupa proclaims, rolling his Rs around the horror as he lances a septic ulcer on Blessing's foot and delicately probes the open wound with a twig.

'Pestilence and disease afflicting the human is everywhere on this God-forsaken continent, but I tell you there is naught so apt a metaphor for the grotesque fecundity of life in Africa as her gut-dwelling flatworm parasites,' he concludes, as he grips the head of the exposed guineaworm infesting Blessing's foot and tugs at it.

'Do you know that once the cousin of this here guinea-worm, the hookworm, burrows into your skin, she swims through the blood in your veins, through the chambers of your heart and up into your lungs, where she tears through the walls and crawls up your throat – secreting juices to stop you coughing her out in your phlegm – so she can get swallowed down into your gut? Then, when she gets into your gut, she bares her nasty great fangs and sinks 'em into your membranes.' Blessing winces as Oupa begins to wind the guineaworm on to the twig.

'What does she do with 'er fangs after she bares them, then?'

'Sinks them into your membranes, Oupa.'

'That's right. An' all the while she's unscathed,' he adds, shaking his head incredulously. 'She secretes a *muti* to suppress your immune system, see, and she can just float right on through your stomach acids that'd liquefy the flesh of a lesser man, like she's bathing in milk.'

Luckily, Cia and I have never been infected with guinea- or hookworm, but we'd be lying our heads off if we said we've always been worm-free. Both of us have had bilharzia. Bilharzia larvae infect the tiny snails that trawl our waterways, biding their time till someone wades in or drinks the water – although since they're fatal to the snail, it's more like a race against time for them to find the next host. You can be hosting thousands and thousands of worms and not even know it, unless you don't get rid of all the eggs in your poo. Then they die and rot inside you causing your belly to bloat up. At the end of every term, the whole school lines up and gets two jabs in the shoulder. Everyone strains to watch the kid up front to see if the second jab swells, which means you've got the worms. Last term both Cia's and mine swelled.

Worms aren't the end of it either. If Philemon, Jobe's helper, doesn't iron the sheets with an iron straight out of

Hell's Inferno, we get putsi fly larvae boils in our backs; the low veld is infested with tsetse fly, which bite like brutes and infect their victims – bovine and human alike – with the deadly sleeping sickness; and there are leeches and blood-bloated ticks. Mom nearly died of tick-bite fever last year. She lay and sweated in her bed for days and me and Cia weren't allowed to make a noise.

Oupa says our tormentors are so copious as to defy reckoning and that it'd be plain futile to even try to destroy such a biological cornucopia. So he narrows his crusade to the bloodthirsty mosquito, since the malaria parasite, which the mosquito alone carries, ranks among the oldest of all human and even pre-human parasites and is a noble and deadly foe. Oupa claims that only the female mosquito, who must have a meal of blood before she can lay eggs, infects humans with malaria. The male is a vegetarian that dines on the nectar of flowers. She hunts us in darkness, when we are most vulnerable, attracted by the aroma of our breath, warm and sweet and moist. With two slender probes, she pierces the skin, with another pair, she saws open the wound and with a third, she sucks out the blood, infecting the sleeping victim with malaria – like in a fairytale, a sort of poisonous kiss.

While Oupa, like the rest of us, has succumbed to the strange dreaming fevers of malaria, Cia and I suspect that his motive for attack is more petty. He just wants to get them for their incessant high-pitched whining and the manically itchy welts their blood anti-coagulant leaves behind. Whatever it is, Oupa devotes himself tirelessly to the task of brewing a deadly repellent. Jobe acts as his chemist, supplying him

50

with a continual stock of ingredients with which to experiment.

'This one, *madala*, is the powerful *muti*,' Jobe claims, as he offers another pungent poultice prepared by the local *n'anga*, who is also a herbalist. Cia and I serve as dual lab assistants and guinea pigs, which is never pleasant since the foundation of every concoction is quinine.

None of them works. Mozzies descend on us in the summer evenings, plunge their syringe-like proboscises into our flesh and drink like vampires, regardless of our blood's quinine concentration. Mom told us that one year, when malaria outbreaks in the district reached epidemic proportions, the government dispatched aerial crop dusters that doused us in DDT, killing the mozzies, poisoning our river, the fish, the birds, and leaving a swathe of death in its wake the like of which will give her nightmares for ever. In the end, the stench of rotting flesh pervaded the whole valley. Oupa says it was a holocaust.

After hearing about Mom's nightmares Cia went to Oupa and stood there lying about his mozzie *muti*. She told him his *muti* worked a treat, and urged him to tell the government that they didn't need to come back ever again.

'Will you tell them, Oupa? Will you tell the gov'ment they don't have to come back here? Not ever. We can take your *muti*, Oupa, and we won't get sick. We won't get sick again, I promise – will we, Nyree?'

One afternoon me and Cia find Mom crying in her room. We'd heard mewling, muffled by the heavy teak door, which we hesitate outside. Cia looks worriedly at me. Mom never closes her door. Eventually I turn the knob and we creep inside, like intruders. Mom is curled up on her bed, her face turned to the wall. She doesn't seem to notice us. I have never seen Mom cry before. Seeing her like this is somehow shocking. We stand there watching her, too afraid to call to her. After a long while, Cia whispers, 'Mom?'

Mom lifts her head and turns to us. Her face is blotchy, her eyes puffy. 'Come here, my loves,' she says, reaching out to us. We rush to her in relief. 'I'm just wallowing in self-pity, don't worry.'

In her hand is a crumpled letter from Dad. I recognize his oversized scrawl on the blue tissue paper.

'Here you go,' she says, holding out the last page to us as we climb on to the bed with her. I study our drawing to see if anything's different. It looks the same as usual: Dad's pointing his rifle. I scan her blotchy face once more, but she is smiling now. 'I just miss your dad, that's all.'

Then she puts her arms round us, one on either side of her, and pulls us close. We lie against the pillows that way for a long time. Mom strokes her fingertips up the pale skin of our inner arms. None of us says anything. I try to keep as still as possible, I don't want anything to rouse her. Then Cia ruins it. She shivers with the tickling and that jolts Mom out of it.

She sighs. 'Sometimes, girls, I wonder if it's all for nothing. We'll probably end up like Zambia, no matter what we do.'

Mom was born in Zambia, except it was called Northern Rhodesia then. Her parents, our grandparents, still live up there, in a town called Kalalushi. At Christmas we go to see them. Mom says it was a wonderful place when she was a child. Cia wrinkles her nose but doesn't say that it sure isn't wonderful any more. Mom sighs all the time when we're there.

Kalulushi is slowly being eaten by greedy plants. It lies on the edge of the Congo basin, beneath the rusting headgear of its abandoned copper mine. One shaft has fallen down and half sunk into the mud. The prying roots of the African flame trees that still line its avenues have torn up the tarmac and it is too dangerous to drive after dark. Most of the houses are vacant, derelict, dark and brooding, the gaping windows like shard-rimmed eyes. Their front gardens grow feral, beneath which, somehow, are still discernible the faded contours of once manicured beds. Grumps and Grandma have helped themselves to the mine captain's house and Mom says they live in faded opulence and borrowed importance, which sounds like old clothes, and it's true, they do wear old things.

Grumpy used to work down the mine. 'Now that's a proper job, that is,' he says.

Dad told us that the mines of the copper belt were once among the richest in the world, and we can still see the glory of the past in the cricket ground with its vine-clotted ruin of a pavilion, the weedy tennis lawns and the rec club with its moth-eaten velvet curtains, tarnished silver in the trophy cabinet and the faint letters on the captains board. Mom used to tell us about the dances in the ballroom and, standing in its dustsheet-draped silence, I can almost hear the tinkling of the ivories on the old Steinway baby grand, the echoes of laughter, the clinking of champagne glasses. It was where Dad met Mom, at one of the dances. Dad was hitch-hiking up from Southern Rhodesia. He says he swept Mom off her feet. The last name on the captains board is Grumpy's. It was engraved in 1964.

I sure hope we don't end up like Zambia. Grumpy and Grandma always squeeze me and Cia goodbye and say they wish we weren't leaving, but I'm kind of glad to leave – it's spooky way up there.

'Come on now, girls. We can't loll around for ever,' Mom says, in her normal voice, then rises and pulls her loose hair back into a ponytail.

6

'Here it is,' Oupa says, with a sorrowful air, 'the very altar upon which they slaughtered the poor wee children to the ravenous gods.' I peer over the rim the better to see the altar where the slaughtering took place. We are standing on a ledge of rock, Oupa, Cia and me, that juts out over a natural amphitheatre. We've come to see the ruins of Great Zimbabwe, which lie just outside Fort Victoria to the south of us, because Dad came home from fighting in the bush and said he didn't want to see any *mombies* or *munts* or goddamned busted pumps, so we left and now we're here, but I don't think that Dad wanted to see us any more either, because he and Mom are gone and we've just got Oupa as our guide.

The ruins of Great Zimbabwe, which stand upon a plateau surrounded by bald-headed granite hills, are stone ghosts that rise from somewhere beneath the earth called antiquity. A vast circular stone wall encloses a tower that spirals like the Tower of Babel hundreds of feet high into the heavens, and in the jungle that grows up a steep hillside close by lies a maze of huge herringbone walls of interlocking stone.

No one knows who built it – the ancient architects have disappeared into the past, leaving no trace of themselves save their masonry. Hundreds of years ago, when the first whispers of a stone palace deep in the heart of Africa reached the coastal trading ports of Mozambique, the Portuguese explorers went exploring, but they never found it so now we'll never know who built it – especially since when the English explorers finally discovered it last century, Oupa says they went and scoured it of the filth and squalor of the *kaffir* occupation. Cia sucks in her breath: we aren't allowed to say the K word.

'Seems like it was the bloody *kaffirs* themselves who built it, though.' He chuckles, then frowns disapprovingly. ''Tis a great shame, though. The scouring left but the vestiges of archaeological evidence in the walls.'

Luckily, though, Oupa knows many details about the fabled Great Zimbabwe that no one else does: Great Zimbabwe was a marvellous medieval kingdom of savages who garnered great wealth from the trading of gold, ivory and slaves with caravans of traders from Arabia. Legend has it that this was where the Queen of Sheba found gold for the Temple of Solomon. And if you listen with your ear against the damp, mossy stone walls you can still hear the pulsating beat of ancient drums in the labyrinth of passages, goading on thousands of naked, frenzied dancers, eyeballs rolling, engorged tongues distended. Standing above the sacrificial altar now, I can hear the echo of children screaming too. Not Cia, though.

'They *never* slaughtered the wee children,' she protests indignantly, and then more hesitantly, 'did they, Nyree?' I look down and am appalled to see what appears to be a row of spear-fashioned stone stakes just right for impaling children.

'Oh, yes, they did,' Oupa assures her grimly. 'The foul savages sacrificed their own children to the flesh-eating gods of the underworld. You are looking at the bloody altar upon which they hurled their young.'

Cia gazes unhappily at the bloody altar upon which the young got hurled.

Afterwards we beg Oupa to let us go to see the *n'anga*. He's stationed mercenarily, Oupa says, just outside the ruins to profit from the gullibility of tourists like Cia and me. But we don't care what class of mercenary he is. The *n'anga* is a diviner who can tell you your fortune.

Cia and I are utterly in the thrall of these men of magic. Oupa says a *n'anga*'s just an oul' charlatan, preying on the superstitions of the *munts* in their benighted ignorance, and he'll nail our pelts to the wall if he catches us dabbling in that voodoo skulduggery. Even Mom and Dad reserve a sort of condescension for witchery. But Cia and I know better.

Over the years, Jobe has taught us much about the powers possessed by the *n'anga*, who is at once a healer, a prophet and a priest, an exorcist and a sorcerer. Above all, the *n'anga* has the power to hear the voices of the dead.

The *n'anga* is chosen by the spirits to speak with those

57

descended from them and it is through the *n'anga* that the living's prayers may be answered. Jobe says that the one who is the creator, the giver of life, and who has many names – 'I have heard Him known as Lezer, in some places, Oluwa, sometimes He is known as Jesus Christ' – is too far away to hear our prayers. I can believe that. At any rate the Holy Spirit doesn't seem to be listening to the long list of things I've asked for in my prayers. So you need your ancestors to ask for you.

But the *n'anga* doesn't just sit around uselessly praying all the livelong day. You can get proper help too, and you don't have to ask for peace and other noble things. The *n'anga* of the village close to our farm is busy from dawn to dusk brewing love potions and talismans to ward off evil, and cures for every kind of ailment. Jobe reckons the *n'anga* is so important he could be in charge of the army, but he's too old. Maybe his son, then.

The cures are cunning too. For instance, lion's fat smeared into your skin will give you courage and strike fear into the heart of your enemies, although Jobe reckons a crocodile is the best – a mighty and magical animal, his teeth grow for ever and his hide can deflect bullets.

The novice *n'anga* is shown first by his *n'anga* teacher and later by his guiding ancestor spirits where to find the particular ingredients to cure an illness, like lizard fat and dried baboon liver, although since most ingredients are just roots and leaves and bark and whatnot, he can pick them in the veld. Even Cia and I could find them without any guidance from ancestor spirits.

The *n'angas'* true gift, though, is not in the treating of ill-ness, but in knowing *why* you fell ill. They alone know what lies behind suffering: the wrath of the ancestors or the evils of witchcraft.

Now, the ancestors sure can get angry for a whole load of reasons – neglect or broken commandments, like fighting between kin – and when they do, sickness and misfortune may follow. But, in truth, it is not their ancestors that people fear, but the far more terrible power of the witch.

Around the fire down by the *khaya*, the Afs dipping into a charred pot of *sadza* and dunking the lumps into another of gravy, we have heard tales of the witches' dreadful deeds. There was a mighty powerful witch who lived in Jobe's vil-lage when he was a boy. At night she rode stark naked on the back of a winged hyena; she blew a magical powder into the wind through a kudu horn, inflicting madness, illness or death. If you looked into her eyes you saw how you were going to die.

'*Hau!*' exclaimed the appreciative crowd. Cia and I gasped.

Right now, Cia and I just want to see the witchdoctor, who has the power to see into your past and what is yet to come.

'Please, Oupa, please please *pleeease?*' Cia begs shame-lessly.

Eventually Oupa grunts and digs in his trouser pocket for a few coins and we are ushered nervously inside the *n'anga's* small beehive-shaped grass hut by a silent, genuflecting apprentice.

Inside, it is sinister, cavernous, dimly lit – we can barely see through the smoke that coils sluggishly from the embers of a small fire in the centre of the room. The air is pungent, the cloying smell of rancid animal blood, curds and ill-cured hide scored through by a potent infusion of the dried herbs that festoon the walls. My nostrils flare. The wizened old *n'anga* is crouched in the middle of the room, like the grisly centrepiece of his grisly pharmacy. Anklets of beads and pods rustle at his bare feet, a headdress of horns and a gnarled staff lie beside him. He is terrifyingly magnificent.

'I am Jabulani.' He introduces himself solemnly and the whites of his eyes are disquieting in the gloom.

Then he holds out a leather pouch containing his divining tools – a collection of small bones, shells and stones. I drop my coins inside and blow over it. Jabulani shakes the bag vigorously and spills its contents on to the pelt in front of him. We lean forward, watching intently, as Jabulani deciphers the messages sent by the ancestors.

'Eh-heh,' he says, nodding sagely as he prods about. 'Eh-heh . . .

'You will have many childrens,' he pronounces at last. 'There will be three boys, one girl. You will have great riches. Your husband will have fat herds, good crops. But one of your children will die. You have no trouble with the police.'

I am nonplussed by my ordinary life. I shrug my disgust. 'Oh.'

Then it is Cia's turn. She blows theatrically into the bag, Jabulani spills its contents on to the floor with a flourish and we lean forward with renewed eagerness. Jabulani casts his hands over the stones, mutters incomprehensibly to himself and then, suddenly, his hand is still. There is a long portentous silence. Then Jabulani inhales deeply on a long pipe nestling in the embers a little to his side. We watch in fascinated horror as his eyes roll into the back of his head and the milky blue whites stare sightlessly at us in the gloom.

'I see the coming of the darkness,' he says hoarsely. 'There is one who will come among you who will bring suffering, and the one will be the jackal. You, you, little one, must not fight the jackal. You are like the mouse – you must run from your enemy, little mouse, run, run for cover.' And Jabulani's dark irises slip down from his sockets. A shiver of dread runs down my spine.

Then he whispers something to his apprentice who shuffles on his knees to the back of the beehive, rummages around in the rusting jam tins and scoured-out calabash pods, then shuffles back to us. Jabulani takes something from him and then turns to offer it to Cia in the same way.

I lean close to her the better to see what's lying on his pink, rutted palm. It is the burned husk of a scarab beetle with a bit of stick tied to its horn with gristle.

'Breathe into this, *ingane*,' Jabulani says, pulling the stick out from what I now see is a tiny hole drilled through the horn. '*Ingane*' is Jobe's special name for Cia. It means 'little one' in Jobe's language, Ndebele.

Cia looks at me – she's not sure if she should give away her breath.

'*Shesha! Shesha!*' Jabulani urges her, and before she has time to think about it again, Cia leans forward and breathes into the hole of the burned scarab. Jabulani quickly plugs it back up with the little peg. Now, he says, Cia can never die. Any time she starts fixing to die, her soul will just fly away, right at that very moment, to the place of her *amadlozi* and she will be safe, and nothing, not the shadows or the owl or anything, can eat up her soul. And Jabulani knows everything about dead people. He presses the scarab into Cia's hand and tells her to keep it safe always.

'I wish you many blessings and good rains.'

Outside we stand blinking as the sun leaches away the spookiness. Oupa is squatting on a granite boulder a short way off, smoking a cigarette he's rolled.

'Well, what'd the old doom-mongering swindler have to say for himself?' he enquires wryly.

Cia turns instinctively away from him as she opens her palm. I am sick with envy. I lean in close to her, but as I reach for the scarab Cia balls her fist and snatches it away. I have the urge to hit her. Then I remember Jabulani's warning about the coming of darkness and my anger evaporates. 'Cia,' I say urgently, 'don't lose that, and remember to beware of a jackal.'

'Okay, I won't. But I'm not scared of some old jackal – he's just *sommer* a wild dog, man.'

'*Ja*, I know, but watch out anyway, just in case. Let's tell Jobe when we get home. He'll know what to do.'

On the way home by the old pass through the Vumba mountains, the dark, brooding canopy of trees bows sombrely over the road. We stop in the early evening at a small lay-by. As we mill aimlessly about while Dad hunkers over the

Landie's radiator, we become slowly aware of a sound permeating through the forest. It filters down to us through the shadows and tranquil light from somewhere above – an ethereal sound of voices raised in song carried on the night-tinged air. We fall silent, straining to hear the muted sound. Eventually, Mom sets off up one of the barely visible pathways that open on to the lay-by. 'Come on,' she calls behind her. 'Let's see where it's coming from.'

Cia and I follow. We don't have far to go, really. A few hundred yards into the forest a humble church huddles in a small clearing, at the base of the lordly trees. Its holiness is discernible only by the whitewash on the wattle-and-daub walls and the crude wooden cross erected over the portals. We congregate in the churchyard and peer into the darkness beyond, from where the music is seeping. Standing before rough-hewn wooden pews, about fifty black worshippers are one in praise of Him.

The sound is unbearably beautiful. It makes me yearn for something. As the voices rise and fall in an outpouring of glory, I feel Cia's breath damp on my cheek. 'Oh, Nyree,' she whispers, 'it's so sad.'

7

The rainy season has begun and the nights, swollen and sullen, are lanced by dark, spiny curtains of rain. It is raining, too, on the day he comes to the Vumba.

Cia and I are out in the garden, sloshing through half a foot of water, collecting snails in a large galvanized pail, for which we earn a cent a snail. There's a fortune to be made this way – the pail is already more than half full – which is why we aren't discouraged by the rain even as it pelts down. Over the din, I hear Mom hollering for us from the back door, and with no alternative but to obey – to ignore her would be perilous – we're obliged to abandon our booty-hunting and stagger back to the kitchen, lugging the pail between us. Jobe is lying in wait for us. As soon as we traipse through the door, he grabs us and roughly towels us off in front of the old cast-iron stove. Then, without further ado, Mom ushers us, clammy and dishevelled, through to the *voorkamer*. As we enter through the archway we halt on cue as our eyes fall upon the stranger.

He is in the middle of the room, standing almost to attention in front of Oupa who is ensconced on an old wingback chair. It is Rapunzel, Cinderella and Snow White's Prince Charming.

'Lasses,' Oupa says, in his most formal voice, 'this is your cousin Ronin. He is to be living with us a while.' He doesn't bother to tell him our names.

Cia is enchanted. She smiles bashfully from behind me – strangers in our midst make her shy. I just stare. This must be the bastard boy, who's somehow turned up in our own *voorkamer*, except Prince Charming looks nothing like the bastard boy of my imaginings – a mixture of Oliver Twist and Dennis the Menace from the *Beano* annuals, on account of his grandfather, a scoundrel and a bounder. Prince Ronin stares back at us, an inscrutable expression on his face.

'How do you do?' he says at last, just as formal. Cia giggles and Oupa says we are dismissed.

Even though we're dismissed we loiter. There are few things as interesting as strangers on the farm, and none so interesting as the ones who look like Prince Charming, are sodden with scandal and disgrace and are real live descendants of Great-uncle Seamus.

We linger in the hallway trying to overhear what Oupa is saying to Ronin. His mutterings are inaudible but I can tell from the high pitch of Mom's voice that she's being especially nice to him. A short while later, the door opens and she escorts Ronin upstairs. We follow Jobe as he carries Ronin's trunk up to the empty bedroom behind Mom and Ronin. After Mom has shown Ronin his room, she leaves him, half closing the door behind her. I glimpse her touching his golden head before she does. She beckons the two of us, dawdling in the passage, into her own bedroom and closes the door.

In a hushed voice she explains that our cousin, who has been away for his first term at boarding-school, has come to stay with us during his holidays, as he will from now on. Cia and I want to know why he got sent away to boarding-school in the first place. I figure it must be because he behaved so badly his mom had to send him away to the torture chambers where they chain you up in the basement most of the time, but Mom says, no, it wasn't that sort of thing, that sometimes people are punished for others' bad behaviour. Cia wants to know if Dad is aware that he got sent to boarding-school even though he wasn't bad. Mom says that he is, but he's busy fighting the Terrs and we are to be nice to our cousin.

We dog his every move.

For the most part Ronin seems rather aloof and he ignores us as studiously as we're studying him. He proves worth the scrutiny. He tears branches from trees and thrashes their trunks. He broods for hours down by the riverine, his hands shoved deep in his pockets, scuffing his shoes through the dirt. It's not long before Cia and I take to mooching about, our hands shoved deep in pretend pockets, brazenly scuffing our shoes through the dirt, in flagrant violation of Mom's shoe-scuffing rules.

Dinnertime seems to bring him around, and he goes back to princely charmingness for a while. We stare agape, until

Mom points out the impoliteness of staring agape at a person, so then we stare closed-mouthed. We're dying to ask him about Great-uncle Seamus, but neither of us has dared to broach the subject yet. In fact, all of our conversations have floundered. From his very first day, when we pretended to stumble upon him while he was unpacking his trunks in his room across the landing from ours it didn't go too well.

I slouched in the doorway, Cia behind me. 'I'm Nyree Angélique O'Callohan,' I said, making up for Oupa's rudeness. 'This here's Cia.'

Cia doesn't have a second name. Her proper name is Ciaran but no one ever remembers that.

Ronin said nothing back.

'I'm eight and three-quarters and I can shoot from a catty. Even baboons . . .'

'So what?'

'I just thought you'd like to know, is all. You need anything shot from a catty, I can do it.'

'You look kinda runty for eight.'

'*Ja*, but I'm growing *sterek* now.'

Ronin shrugged.

'Do you wanna see the house, then? Me and Cia'll show you, if you want. It's called Modjadji, you know.'

Ronin shrugged again, but he got up off his knees to follow us. We descended the stairs so as to start with the grandest rooms, the hall, the dining room, the library, but as we moved from one to the next, Ronin seemed less and less impressed. His lip curled as he appraised the walls, which have burped and sagged with damp, the russet lace blooming

68

on the paintings, the fogged clocks, the white dandruff drifting from the beams, furry with fungus and quivering with termites.

Eventually, in a desperate bid to impress, Cia pointed to the cabinet in the *voorkamer* behind whose thick opaque glass is the great dust-coated Bible, locked away for its holiness. 'There's a *gun* in there, you know,' she said in an awed tone.

Ronin just looked at her, but Cia was hopeful. She groped behind the fire grate where the key is hidden. The gun is stowed behind the Bible, which sits on an easel, very old and holy, the gold letters gleaming on the dark worn leather. It first belonged to Christiaan de Beer, who was a Protestant. He came to Africa with the other Protestants because the Catholics had merciless priests in cruel crimson robes burn them at the stake for not believing that the bread and wine of Holy Communion magically turn into the body and blood of Christ. Oupa says the air was thick with the smell of charred Protestants so there was an Exodus, like in Genesis, to Africa, which was the Promised Land.

Christiaan landed at the Cape of Storms in 1692 aboard the Dutch East India Company ship *Vryburg*. That he lived and died is layered between the sombre, velvety-penned words: '*In den Namen God*' and '*Soo waarlyk helpe my God Almagtig Amen*'.*

Oupa says he lies buried in an old churchyard nestled in the vineyards of Franschoek, where the Afrikaners lived

*'In the name of God. So truly help me God Almighty, Amen.'

until they went on the Great Trek. They had to venture forth into the dark heart of Africa with nothing but their ox-wagons, their Fortitude and their Faith in God Almagtig. Although Oupa reckons it amounted to nothing more than a few mongrel Dutchmen snivelling away from the stranglehold of British imperialism with their wretched spans of slaves lashed to their ox-wagons, along with their Fortitude and Faith.

I wonder if Christiaan has a sinking, moss-eaten tombstone and if it is engraved with the words '*Soo waarlyk helpen my God Almagtig Amen*'. But since Ronin didn't even care about the gun, I knew we might as well not bother with his Bible.

I wished we could get into the attic where our dead grandmother's belongings are hidden. But Oupa holds them sacred, and since he suspects that we're just dying to get our filthy little grave-robbing mitts on them on account of not having so much as a shred of decency between us, we're not to go near the place – so the attic is her shrine, a shrine visited by no pilgrims.

Things haven't got much better with Ronin since then. In the way of striking up a conversation, we don't get past taking out the match.

'Hi, Ronin. Whatcha doing, hey?'

'Nothing.'

'Oh.'

A pause.

'Do you want to see the chicken coop? There's new baby chicks just hatched.'

'No.'

'Oh. Uh. Okay, then.'

A longer pause.

We share our bathroom with him now. We have to knock before we open the door. Ronin owns a toothbrush, a tube of toothpaste and a comb. They're lined up on the shelf above ours in the vanity cupboard that's mounted over the basin; ramrod straight in a row. Even his toothpaste tube is carefully folded up from the bottom, not squashed in the middle and oozing toothpaste like ours. He probably doesn't like the toothpaste we leave glooped all over the basin either. Those toilet soldiers seem kind of odd.

Looked at more closely, his Prince Charmingness cheapens a little. He still looks princely all right, but he's like a blond boy Barbie doll and there is something faintly girlish in his chin – an impression accentuated by vanity. The way he keeps sweeping the blond lock of hair from his brow is what Oupa calls precious, in a mean, mealy-mouthed way. Only Ronin's eyes are truly distinctive. Their blue is so pale as to be grey, almost see-through, and when he looks right at me, through me, which isn't often, they make me feel somehow apprehensive. They remind me of Nosferatu, who flickered eerily across our black and white TV one night, until Cia and I were caught hiding behind the couch and sent to bed. They are Great-grandfather's colourless, polite eyes.

For Cia though, what Ronin's lost in princeliness he's made up for in pitifulness. As far as she's concerned Ronin really is the Dickensian tale come to life of the abandoned half-orphan boy who was banished to the torture chambers, and though he is much bigger and older than us, she feels keenly sorry for him and smiles earnestly at him whenever she gets a chance. I know it costs her to do so, she's shy in those ways, but she exerts herself for his sake. She is not rewarded.

While he never plain snubs her, he never smiles back either, and it seems to me that it isn't entirely on account of awkwardness. It's the way he stares at her for a moment. He doesn't blush or bridle, just stares. In fact, away from the riverine, everything about him seems deliberate. Around the adults, he is pleasant. It's a wishy-washy sort of word and that's the way he is – always pleasant, but only pleasant, as if he's wearing a mask of pleasantness. It makes me uneasy. And his silky voice, even his posture, seems as contrived as his expression. As the days pass, he reins in something inside himself too. The tree thrashing stops, and we never glimpse anything so raw in Ronin again.

To be fair, his pleasantness with Mom seems genuine, as if he's anxious to please her, but with Oupa it's forged. For a start he pretends as if he can't wish for anything better to do of an afternoon than listen to Oupa's gin-curried sermons on the *stoep*, and he makes the mistake of trying to let Oupa know it by interrupting all the time with little compliments and agreeing with him too eager-like.

'Our great-grandfather was obviously a fine man, sir, and if I may say, sir, his son must have made him proud.'

This sure doesn't endear him to Oupa. Every afternoon he ends up telling Ronin a little earlier than the day before that his faggoty coquetry, whatever faggoty coquetry is, makes him sick to his gut, until Ronin takes to avoiding the afternoon sittings altogether. We are half envious. He still doesn't dodge Oupa completely, though.

Late one afternoon as he half slinks, half stalks, hyena-like, round the corner, Oupa pounces on him. 'Oi, you, boy! Have yer finished yer chores yet?'

Ronin starts, but quickly regains his composure. He flicks his lock of hair off his forehead nervously. 'Yes, sir, finished them all, sir.'

He's not lying. Ronin does his chores like a goody-goody. It's not for Oupa, though, that he does them. It's for Mom.

She gave him his chores, said he was old enough to help out more on the farm and that she was pleased to have a boy around. Ronin reckons he's the man about the place, the way he swaggers around chewing on a grass stalk like Dad does. He only does it when Dad's gone, though.

He does them all real carefully too, his chores, even the sissy ones, like sewing the *mielie* sacks closed with the special *mielie* needle. He sat there frowning with his tongue poking out of the side of his mouth, sewing them up as neat as if he were darning socks. Then he showed Mom, like he always does, pretending to check that he was doing it right, and went pink when she told him how good he was doing it. Sometimes she even ruffles his hair or pats him. Cia doesn't like to see that either. I watch her watching with slitty eyes.

Anyway, even though it's true that he's done them, Oupa ignores him. 'Because we don't tolerate wastrels and slackers round these parts. You'll earn yer keep along with everyone else here.'

'Yes, sir. You won't catch me idling, sir. Have you any more chores for me, sir?' His voice is milky.

Somehow this seems to incense Oupa. His jaw juts a little more, he eyes Ronin with his hereditary Latin imperiousness for a moment, then adds, 'No. And parasites what arse-creep are still parasites, just browner.'

For a moment Ronin looks stricken, before he manages to rearrange his face. *Parasite* cuts like a knife through a soft thing. Cia looks down at the now flushed parasite, positively anguished. At that moment Mom steps outside. She breathes in the air that has sponged up the poison and demands to know what's going on. No one answers, so she disbands the gathering on the spot. 'And don't pay any heed to him,' she adds, looking quizzically at Ronin while nodding towards Oupa. She seems to include us in that too.

After that incident, Ronin gives up trying to win Oupa's approval, but he goes on swallowing Oupa's tongue-lashings, which Oupa regularly doles out. Why Oupa does it, Cia and I don't know, but he savours his disapproval of Ronin, chewing it like a wad of tobacco, rolling it around with his tongue. We heard Mom shouting at Oupa about it one night after dinner. She asked him what sort of a sadistic old sod inflicts such cruelty on a child, said he couldn't lay all the blame on Seamus and that it was time to grow up, which was a funny thing to say to an old man. But Oupa always tells us that an O'Callohan 'never borrows, never begs' and Ronin's fawning is too much for him to bear.

Why Ronin submits so meekly to it is even more unfathomable, but at the same time he bears unmistakable contempt towards us. He still says little to Cia or me, or anyone else for that matter, but when we are alone, his facial expression, normally so carefully composed, slips into something more akin to a sneer. This is true for the Africans too. Slowly Cia stops smiling at him and begins to look wary when he appears. She still suffers a paroxysm of pity for him when Oupa takes to humiliating him, but her and my feelings for him are becoming more ambivalent.

8

Cia and I are out on the front lawn doing a vigorous performance of 'Baby Makes Her Blue Jeans Talk'. We only know the chorus, though, so we have to sing it over and over, which is getting on Oupa's nerves so bad that if he has to hear our execrable rendition of it one more time he's gonna come down off that *stoep* and send our unbaptized backsides straight to hell all bloated with sin.

'She don't say nothin', but baby makes those blue jeans talk,' yells Cia, energetically wiggling her bum behind me.

Oupa wants to know whether she is aware that hell is teeming with devils who have nothing better to do all day than stab her *in* the bum with hot pitchforks. If Cia is aware she doesn't care, since 'Baby Makes Her Blue Jeans Talk' is still a whole heap better than the Lone Ranger, which is what we were doing till Cia announced that she's sick to her guts of being cast as Tonto and refused to play it any more even though I offered her Hi Ho Silver instead. Luckily for her bum, though, Jobe hollers from the kitchen for us to come inside and get washed. We wiggle our way to the back door and slouch around rebelliously just outside it.

'*Aah*, why must we?' Cia sasses insolently.

'Because you going to sleep in town and you can't go making your *mamie* ashamed wearing that filth,' Jobe informs us.

We perk up immediately. Sleeping in town? *Mush*.

It turns out that an auction's being held. Auctions are just by themselves *mushi sterek*, taking place in a great din of noise and dust inside huge arenas, which you look down on from the mezzanine balcony that spirals around the walls above the arena floor, as great sweating *mombies* stampede in and out – but a night in town is *mushest* of all.

After we've been brutally wiped down by Jobe, twisting and bucking all the while, Dad shoves a comb down one of his long socks and orders us into the back of the Landie with Ronin for the long journey to Umtali. We're both excited but I can't let the over-excitement get to me since if there is so much as one bit of disgracefulness involving either Cia or me, so help her God, Mom will kill us on the spot and we'll be shovelling coals for all eternity.

We are staying at the home of friends – although it should be made plain that it is strictly the parents who are friends. Louis and his brother André are a year each older than me and Cia, plus they have a dead mom. She was killed because of the War. Mrs Schalkwyk was her name.

'Nyree, do you reckon they have to go to her grave?'

'*Ja*. I reckon they have to go there and pray for her immortal soul and stuff.'

I picture Louis and André standing in the grey drizzle, heads bowed by their mother's graveside. I know it's sinful, but I think Heaven sounds boring, with boring old cherubs floating around on clouds playing harps and bugles and whatnot. I don't want to go there.

They have a stepmother now (but not like the one in Cinderella – their one looks like an ordinary kind of mother), and they are townies, which we are not. Our acquaintance with Louis and André goes back a long way, and its sole purpose – a task of which neither ever tires – is for them to remind us of this fact.

Over the years, me and Cia have come to the sad realization on these brief sorties into town that there are certain shaming aspects to living out in the *bundu*. It's the toilet that explains matters best. The bog on the farm is kind of creepy – dank, crawling with *gogos*, with a rusty old chain that dangles just out of reach from the tank mounted high on the wall. It even hosts a bat colony in the eaves, and the paper is pages from the *Farmers' Weekly* cut into squares and hung on a nail – but we didn't notice its creepiness before. At Louis and André's though, it's not even called the toilet. It's called the loo and it's all shiny and white with a knitted pink poodle sporting a pom-pom tail squatting on the spare Fairy toilet roll. The toilet lid has a matching frilly pink hood and there are Kaylite mermaids and goldfish climbing up the walls. Cia and I keep pretending to need the loo so we can go in there again. And we know our bog is downright shameful.

There is a whole lot of other things in the general class of refinement of which *bundu*-dwellers are deprived, but finding out about them involves suffering the sneering and jeering from Louis and André as soon as they detect our ignorance – and, like rats, they can sniff out *bundu* ignorance. It's worth it, though.

Last time we came into town, we found out about the ice-cream boy. We were whirring along a bike track one afternoon on bikes-converted-to-motorbikes with cardboard pegged to the spokes, the jacarandas a purple haze above us, behind Louis, André and a posse of townies. They only let us follow them if we stayed at least two jacarandas behind André, who had to ride last. My shirt was just starting to stick to my back when we heard his bell ringing. By the time Cia and I caught up, the townie boys were huddled around him, big and official in his Dairy Maid uniform in the middle of the mob. We hung back so we'd know how to copy them when it was our turn. At last it was.

'Can I have a tickey-lolly, please?' I asked timidly.

'Can I also have a tickey-lolly, please?' Cia almost whispered.

He smiled like a genie, his teeth luminous against his ebony skin, and opened the lid of his box. A cloud of dry-ice smoke billowed up from its depths, which was like the Arctic in your face, and we peered through it to the treasure trove within. As soon as we each had our mitts on a tickey-lolly we – again in imitation of the townies' technical skill – blew into the wrapper to loosen it. It puffed up satisfyingly and then we were sucking noisily on the neon orange ice.

We tell this story over and over to the other pitifully ignorant *bundu*-dwellers at our school.

'So like, any time, like just on your way home from school, you'll stumble across him just sauntering down the road with a cool box chock full of ice-cream?' asks Dell for the thousandth time, shaking his head incredulously.

'*Ja!* And there's a bi-scope that you can just go to any ol' time you like, and we saw *The Lone Ranger*, which is a million times better than the Jesus ones they show in the school hall,' Cia throws in.

'*Ag!* You lie, man!' Jeremiah, the sceptic, heckles from the back of the crowd.

'I do not!' retorts Cia, all indignant. 'You're just a *plaas-jaapie* who stinks of manure and who's never even been to town and who doesn't know nothing.'

When we get to Louis and André's, though, it's back to *gammadoolah* shame.

André tells Cia that it's painfully obvious to him that she's never clapped eyes on a pogo-stick in her whole *plaas-jaaping* life as Cia loses her balance and falls to the ground yet again. But even as she scrambles to her feet, pretending not to have injured herself, it's not as bad as usual, since this time we've brought Ronin with us, who is indisputably fourteen, which is better than any pogo-stick. And when I tell them – after they've crossed their hearts and hoped to die if they ever tell – that Ronin is an orphan whose father was shot in a skirmish with a *kaffir* and who ran away from reform school where they chain you up in the basement and torture you for hours and hours, it's a revelation that moves Louis to eye us with the beginning of respect.

Since Ronin himself does not acknowledge their existence,

81

they're even more impressed by him and take to plotting ways of getting him out in public where he will be seen by their friends.

'It's sort of like making a mole come out of his hole,' says Louis.

'How's that?' I ask.

'You stick a hose from your exhaust pipe down it and start the engine,' explains André, helpfully.

'If you stick anything down any exhaust pipes I'm telling,' says Cia, 'and exhaust-piping moles is mean.'

''Snot mean, just convinces him to make his molehills in someone else's garden, stupid,' André sneers.

'Not if the other end of his tunnel is blocked it doesn't, and how'd you like to be a mole that got exhaust-piped to death, hey?'

'Jeez, man, I'm just sayin' that we've got to coax him, is all.'

But Mom saves Louis having to do any coaxing, about which I was dubious anyway, by volunteering Ronin to chaperon us to the swimming-baths the very next day. Swimming-baths sound so glamorous, I keep imagining Hollywood synchronized swimmers wearing frilly bathing caps. I'm a bit nervous about going to them actually, but I'm already savouring the recounting to Dell, Jeremiah and the rest so I am excited too, despite Ronin's unmistakable surliness on the way there, past the avenues of neat townie lawns bordered with hibiscus hedges, drooping in pendulous flowers.

Before we arrive at the gates under the imposing arches,

Louis and André are careful to explain that we are not to speak to them and we are not to come near them. We are not to bother them to play Springboks-versus-Lions or anything else embarrassing that is only permitted in the privacy of their back garden. We queue patiently with hordes of other small swimmers for three o'clock – the baths are closed between twelve and three, the hottest hours of the day. Louis and André yell greetings up and down the line, Cia and I are apprehensively quiet and Ronin is sullen. Finally the gate opens, we hand over our five cents and I get flustered trying to propel myself coolly through the turnstile contraption.

From the top of the stairs, Cia and I survey the dazzling turquoise pools that lie before us. The contemptible baby pool is immediately in front of us, the Olympic main pool behind it, the high-dive board soaring above the far end. Palm trees and lush lawns flank both sides. I am intimidated, but trying to act nonchalant, and I feel sorry for Cia, who I know is quaking in her boots. Louis and André lead the way to 'their' tree, where their friends are already waiting.

'This is Ronin. He's *fourteen*!' They introduce our cousin proudly. The posse gazes admiringly at Ronin, who looks deeply scornful.

'We had to bring them,' Louis says, hoicking his thumb over his shoulder at us.

Then, having dispensed with the niceties, the whole posse races to dive-bomb into the pool yelling, 'Geronimo!' at the top of their lungs.

I take a deep breath, clasp Cia's hand in mine and head

for the shallow end – the baby pool is regrettably out of the question. The shallow end is embarrassingly populated by smaller kids, some even accompanied by their moms, and far fewer boys. Geronimo's dive-bombers, however, are bless-edly conspicuous by their absence. We tentatively lower ourselves over the side into the cool depths and instantly my fear is gone. Cia suddenly remembers that she is part amphibious and soon we are torpedoing through the brilliant blue water. We head out deeper and deeper until we encounter the boys, who are in the middle of a breath-holding competition. Louis even lets us in.

Eventually, when the tips of our fingers are puckered, we clamber out and head for the tearoom. The floor is, like nearly all other floors, polished red cement, and now wet and fit for slippering across. We queue behind red-eyed, sopping boys, hair plastered to their scalps, all wanting pink marsh-mallow fish, or yellow bananas, or packets of sherbet with a liquorice straw. Afterwards we are allowed to lie on the grass in the sun with the boys and drink bottles of cream soda through a straw while tearing strips off pink marshmallow fish with our teeth, until they embark on a skins-versus-shirts cricket match.

The shadows are elongating and the afternoon light is treacle when Louis declares that we'd better have our last swim before home-time. Cia and I get up and veer towards the middle end this time. I stand teetering on the edge, chicken-skinned and half reluctant to submerge myself in the now chilly depths, but Cia rises unhesitatingly on tiptoe and dives cleanly into the water. She disappears for a moment beneath the surface. What with the sulphurous chemicals, human debris and shadows, the water seems murkier, and hundreds of kids, like flotsam and jetsam, are still churning it up. Then I see her emerge, hair plastered over her face, and shake the water from her eyes, laughing. Suddenly, though, her expression changes: it registers shock and then she is wrenched under.

I stand bewildered, my heart in my throat, then plunge in after her. Beneath the surface I open my eyes to the searing chlorine and peer through the cloudy water. I can see nothing but kicking legs, through which I fight my way. Someone kicks me right in the face. I swallow gallons of water, which singes the back of my nostrils, and black spots mushroom before my eyes, but I plough on towards where Cia went down. I see what may be thrashing, twisted bodies ahead but I can't be sure. Then I reach out and feel what I know is Cia grab hold of me.

We rise quickly to break the surface. Cia is choking and gasping, her eyes huge, the pupils dilated. I look around wildly. I am confused, panicked, and then somehow I look straight across on a diagonal to the far side of the pool. There is Ronin, squarely in my line of vision, and he is staring directly at us. He holds my gaze for a suspended moment, then turns and pulls himself smoothly from the pool. In that instant, I know it was him.

Cia and I struggle back to the side and I drag her from the water. We sit for a moment while the heaving of her chest subsides.

'I don't know what happened, Nyree, I don't know.

Someone pulled me down and . . . held me down there. They had their hand on my head – I couldn't breathe.' Tears well in her eyes. I put my arm round her shoulders to comfort her, but I am spooked too.

Afterwards I doubt what I saw with my own eyes. It was so momentary that I can't even be sure I saw Ronin in the water – the way he'd pulled himself from it, like he was lubricated. It was surreal in the midst of my panic. Afterwards it was as though he was never there – and even if he was, that doesn't mean he did it to Cia. Why would he? I try to dismiss it.

On the way home, Cia is subdued, I feel uneasy, but Ronin seems nothing more than his normal slightly haughty self. He gives nothing away, and eventually Louis and André's boisterousness buoys our mood a little. We walk the rest of the way trying to trip each other up at the ankles.

I don't tell Cia my suspicions and she seems to forget about it soon enough. In fact, she seems to take especial delight in the telling of the tale – only slightly embellished – of the swimming-baths to Dell and the other kids from our farm district when we get home. 'Man, you've never seen a pool so deep – it's deeper than the Atlantic ocean. It's so deep that if you hold your breath and swim down for a mile you still won't reach the bottom. *Hey*, Nyree?'

But I don't forget – I can't quite deceive myself.

9

It's not long after the swimming-baths – we're still milking the whole swimming-bath jamboree, actually – and me and Cia are sitting on the back-door steps peeling-and-licking and squashing peanut butter and jam sandwiches. Jobe is standing a little way off, just inside the entrance to the laundry, his arms elbow deep in the churning, foaming washing-machine.

Mom says it's a relic that predates the bloody twin-tub and calls it the great garrulous tank. The great garrulous tank lost its lid years ago, so it shudders and slops soapsuds all over the floor as it churns the laundry. Cia and I like to plunge our arms into it, but we've been forbidden today on account of peanut butter and jam stickiness, although Jobe has graciously consented to decant some of the murky green soapsud potion into a vial for us instead – to be used in an upcoming Fairyland-flight attempt. In the tank are the waters of the great grey-green greasy Limpopo river, all set about with fever trees – they're bound to be magic.

Jobe often panders to us in a way that no one else will, in the way of the soapsud potion, indulging our fatuous fairy fantasies and other rot and drivel, Oupa says. I suspect that it's half because we pander to Jobe, too, by being the audience for his life story, which he likes to tell in garish detail as he works. Jobe doesn't have only one life story, though: he has lived many, many lives. Me and Cia squat on the floor and listen to them and clap in the good bits. The best bit is when Jobe was Jobe the Gold Miner.

When he was a young man, still living with his tribe in the place of his birth near Kwa Bulawayo – the Place of the Slaughter – Jobe was lured into the pay of the great mining houses of Johannesburg, far to the south. In those days, Jobe says, the mines hungered for men. Africa fed the hunger. Like a column of ants the men came to eGoli – the City of Gold – there to be swallowed down the gaping throat of the mines.

The column of ants had been on the march for a long, long time, since the time of Jobe's grandfather, when somebody called Wenela arrived in Jobe's village in the year that he came of age – Oupa reckons that 'Wenela' is how the letters standing for Witwatersrand Native Labour Association got corrupted north of the Limpopo. Jobe tells us how the young men of his village who'd followed Wenela before him returned home at the end of each year laden with great trunks of army knives, mirrors, blankets, ready-made *mielie-meal* and bicycles that came from a place called Jew Stores at the mines – I reckon it's like Aladdin's cave – as well as a wealth of tales that made the teller a hero, worshipped by the smaller boys, and more than enough money to pay *lobola* for a bride.

'Me, I was wanting the Jew Stores and the stories and the *lobola*, hmm-hmm,' Jobe admits.

He signed Wenela's contract.

'Then they give us the PT.'

The PT, we have worked out, was a pair of white PT shorts and a white PT vest.

'After the PT, Oom Gert he lock us up,' Jobe tells us indignantly.

Cia and I look indignant too. Oom Gert and his son were Afrikaners. They took the paper where Jobe had made his mark, and as soon as he was in his PT, they coaxed him into their truck, where they manacled him to a rail lest fear grip his heart and change it in the night. There would be no reneging on his agreement.

The next night, cloaked in darkness, he and the other young ones who'd placed their mark on the paper set forth on their clandestine journey to eGoli, since it was actually Against the Law for Wenela to be recruiting in Rhodesia back then. When the truck arrived at the central depot deep in Matabeleland, he and the other recruits were herded into a huge camouflaged army tent, where they stood in long lines to have a strange metallic coin placed over their hearts.

'If the heart, if the breath, is no good, then you are no good. And the *umlungu udokotela* know. *Eh-heh!* He has the *umshini* that can listen into your heart, into your breath, and know what is to come. And if the *udokotela* say there is something wrong, they say, "*Hamba!*" – "Go!" – and you must go home.'

Something wrong with your breathing means TB. Cia and I know all about TB from Oupa, who is a TB expert. The coin betrayed the symptoms of the disease while it was still secreted in the soft polyps of the lungs.

Having passed his test, though, Jobe was not cast out. He journeyed on, first by road, then river and finally rail, everything everywhere branded 'WNLA'. The number of young men in his company swelled at each station.

'We sing through the night. "Wenela is our father and mother. Wenela the all-knowing will get us there."'

When the great city finally appeared in a mirage on the horizon, Jobe knew fear. The place they call the Reef is an endless black pit strewn with the great iron *umshini* beasts that snarl and hiss and spew smoke and rage. Black blood pumps through their veins, theirs are the sinews of war, and their jaws can crush a man's bones like they're a chicken's. Only at night are they silenced. Although they haven't really fallen silent: if you listen carefully outside the factories where they are chained up, you can hear them – not growling but weeping.

Jobe was immediately delivered by Wenela to the Rand Central Deep mine and into the Compound. In the Compound, where he and hundreds of other miners ate, slept and lived as brothers for the time of their binding contracts, he found an *induna* of the Ndebele. This was good: he would watch over him. The white *baas* of the Compound was known far across the land to be the greatest compound *baas* of all the *izimayini*. He heard the men of other compounds try to lay claim to this honour, but they were just liars.

He was issued with boots, a helmet and strange garb that would protect him down in the darkness of the mines, and then his initiation began. Initiation was to learn 'Fanagolo', known also as 'Chilapalapa', 'Mine Kaffir', 'Pidgin Bantu' and a host of other such names. It is a crossbreed language of Zulu, English, Afrikaans, Portuguese and several others, made up so that the legions of Shangaan from Portuguese East Africa, the Tonga from Malawi, the Basotho from Lesotho and the rest of the fifty tribes working on the mines have a common tongue.

'There was the training,' Jobe informs us gravely. He chants from memory: '*Hamba lusa! Hamba fasa! Eish!*' He shakes his head. 'We spend the *whole* day doing "*Hamba lusa! Hamba fasa!*"'

And the three of us stand in line on the lawn, solemnly chanting, '*Hamba lusa! Hamba fasa!*' in unison and pulling up-and-forwards, down-and-backwards on great imaginary levers, turning the *umshini* on and off.

And then it was over. On his first day and every day thereafter, a siren went off in the compound at two o'clock in the morning when his shift began. It wailed through the darkness into his dreams. He and the thousands of other compound inmates staggered from their slumber to form great queues outside the shafts in the shadow of the towering steel headgear, shuffling forward slowly in the bitter cold of the winter night.

'*Hau!* That place is cold!' It was enough to turn the *ubudoda* – the manhood – into a small boy's.

He shuffled through the brittle cold until it was his turn to climb into the hoist cage and the white hoist driver lowered him down the gorge of the mine.

Jobe worked level twenty-three, and on its descent, the cage would rattle past twenty-two other great gaping holes left by those who had gone before him. The old, abandoned tunnels, propped up by beams, stretched eerily away into the darkness. Down below on the main drive, three thousand feet below the surface of the earth, Jobe described Oupa's Hell. The Realm of the Damned.

Deep inside the bowels of the earth, it is ferociously hot and the air is foul as it coils through your nostrils. It is almost pitch dark as the weak pools of light strung along the rough tunnel roof are gnawed at the edges by a darkness so thick, so viscous, it is a thing, and in the background there is the relentless throb and whine of jackhammers boring into the rockface, pumps working frantically to staunch rising underground floodwaters and the beating of the blades of the massive ventilation fans. Like tortured animals.

Because the gold seams are only inches high, the miners were paid bonuses to crawl into narrow, steeply inclined stopes off the main drives, and work all day in their confines, hacking out the ore and dumping it into the coco-pans that rattled past below. The first time Jobe crawled into his crevice, he choked – in the darkness, with the weight of the rock crushing down on him, crushing the air out of his lungs, he couldn't breathe. Like being buried alive. The veterans knew how to deal with it and, in time, Jobe did too – he even came to find his narrow cleft comforting. And all the while the white foremen patrolled up and down lashing out randomly at the mine boys with their *sjamboks*.

At two o'clock in the afternoon, the sirens would sound the end of the shift and he'd trudge back to the hoist where he'd queue, sometimes for two hours, to be pulled back to the surface.

At night, barricaded into the compound, he joined the throngs of gumboot dancers. Jobe was a champion gumboot dancer in his day – and he likes to boast about it. While Jobe's boasting, me and Cia flail about on the lawn, stomping and slapping our imaginary gumboots. Jobe says we're the worst gumboot dancers he's ever seen, but I reckon if we had real gumboots we could be pretty good.

Other nights, if he was too tired for gumbooting, he just squatted in a circle with other mine boys, smoking and talking. Sometimes there were wild nights in the shebeens, but not often: if you were caught after curfew by the *amaphoyisa*, the swine, with no pass, they dragged you straight to *ijele*. Jobe avoided those dens of iniquity because visits to them frequently ended in ill-fortune. There were dice and women who could make your money vanish, and even if you left with some of it still in your pocket, you could be ambushed on the way home, robbed and beaten to a bloody pulp.

Sometimes they put on film shows in the compound. Jobe liked the hard-riding westerns, but the educational films about mine safety, starring a *mampara* – the Fanagalo word for a dimwit – who did everything wrong, were funny as all-get-out. And then, in the pit of the night, the siren would sound again.

But that was long ago. Since then long talons have been gouged around the edges of his eyes and Jobe is as old as the oldest *umkhulu* in his tribe was when he died. He is singing now as he churns the washing. Jobe has a deep, melodious voice and the sound washes over us as we sit swaying on the stone step. His song is neither a hymn nor a war cry, but a rhythmic, hypnotic chant.

Something makes me glance up, and I see Ronin crouching by the edge of the *stoep* corner, like a rat who knows instinctively that it is vermin, watching furtively. I have noticed before in him the same eerie stealth, the ability to keep very still and very quiet. He is unaware that he himself is being watched, and in the lap of his imagined privacy he wears a sly look. Then he must have felt my gaze on him because he swivels and our eyes touch. Reflexively he casts about guiltily, but then his slippery face resolves itself into defiance. I observe his eely, shifting expression as though from a distance. His posture, which always hovers between cringing and swaggering, swings into swagger. Cia and Jobe see him approach and stiffen. Ronin walks right up to the laundry entrance.

'Doing women's work again, then, hey, Jobe?' he taunts.

It is a grave insult. I am mortified, mute, but Jobe is elderly, imperturbable as befits an elder, and is not about to be roused by petty provocation. He sniffs disdainfully.

Ronin is not so easily deflected, though. He stares impassively at Jobe. Then he places the heel of his boot against the base of the tank and deliberately kicks it over. The ancient machine crashes to the floor, spilling the sodden, soiled clothes and gallons of polluted water.

'Now get down on your knees, *gogo*,' he underscores the word, which means 'old woman', 'and mop up that fucking mess.'

Jobe stares at him, stares right into his eyes. Water cascades around them and down the steps. The machine continues to shudder torturously in its death throes. Ronin shifts almost uncomfortably. No one utters a word. Finally, Jobe shakes his head, almost imperceptibly, his face shutters and he kneels to salvage the washing.

Ronin is gloating. 'And next time I ask you a question,' his voice is dripping spite, 'you stupid old *kaffir*, you answer, "Yes, master," or we'll have another little lesson in humility.' He leans over the bowed Jobe, spits on the floor and strides off. His spittle sits smugly in a little puddle on the floor, frothy, noxious.

Cia and I remain petrified for a moment longer until Cia's outrage revives her. Tears spring to her eyes and she kneels next to Jobe, trying clumsily to shove the washing back into the machine. 'Don't worry, Jobe, I'll do it for you. Don't worry.' She stumbles over her words in her haste to put everything right.

'Leave it, *ingane*. I'll do it,' Jobe rebuffs her gently.

She looks anxiously at him, but gives in for fear of making things worse. She kneels helplessly next to him, mostly in the way, while he resurrects the washing-machine.

'I'm sorry, Jobe. I'm sorry about your washing,' I offer inadequately.

'We'll make *him* say sorry!' says Cia fiercely. 'Won't we, Nyree? He's not allowed to talk to you like that, is he, Nyree? He's not allowed to talk to *any*body like that!'

'No. No, you won't,' says Jobe, ponderously. 'You leave it now. No good will come of this.'

I can see he hasn't dissuaded Cia. No good will come of leaving it either, as far as she's concerned.

'Some hate because it is living in their own skin they hate,' he adds. Then he tells us that he wants no more help and sends us away.

Cia's rage is untamed, though, and she is determined to shame Ronin. We head straight for our forest hideout to plot Jobe's revenge. The deep shade pacifies Cia a little. She is still angry but, her faith in my ability to avenge injustice immutable, she is content to look expectantly at me.

If it is years that have taught Jobe the futility of punishing hatefulness born of hating your own skin, or merely the futility of trying to defend yourself from a position of weakness, Cia hasn't yet learned the lessons. I've worked it out, though, and can think of nothing better than telling on him. I know I'm being a yellow-bellied coward, but I shrink inside when I think of standing up to him – and what for anyway? The sad truth is that me and Cia are ranked bottom of the house – and Ronin knows it. So, while telling tales is the act of a traitor, we decide that since Ronin is already the enemy, it doesn't count.

When we track down Mom out by the feed warehouse, Cia is even more eager than me to rat him out. I try to tell Mom what happened, but Cia keeps interrupting to corroborate and helpfully recap the most atrocious bits. Our story spills out in a confused Babel of voices.

'Mom, Ronin kicked over the washing-machine.'

'He did, Mom, he did! On purpose. And he called Jobe names,' Cia interjects.

'And he swore, Mom.'

'He said the K word,' Cia hisses, then pauses for dramatic effect.

We both look expectantly at her.

'I beg your pardon?' is all she manages. After we have repeated our story several times, and she's interrogated us about whether or not we're telling the truth, the whole truth and nothing but the truth, so help us, God, she dismisses us with 'That's quite enough now. Off you go, you two. It's got nothing to do with you, and I don't want to hear any more about this ugliness.'

But Cia is mollified. Things Mom classifies as 'ugliness' meet with dire consequences. Justice will certainly be meted out and we discharge ourselves.

Later, in the evening, as Cia and I are ambling along the track towards the farmhouse after a soothing afternoon in the riverine collecting tadpoles, we come across Ronin again. I doubt it is accidental. His face is contorted into a kind of a stricken sneer. Mom's obviously been teaching him about what sort of ugliness she doesn't want to see and I can tell we're going to pay for his lesson. I knew it even as we ratted him out; it was a recklessly gratifying thing to do. Now we've sullied him in the eyes of the one person whose love he most desires. I know secretly that that's partly why I did it – I don't want Mom to love him. I watch the way he watches her, the way his eyes never leave her, the hunger in their watery depths, and I don't like it. Now we've sealed our enmity.

Ronin wastes little time.

'Do you know what happens to little girls who tell lies to their mummies?' he asks. Like an animal, my senses are heightened. I can smell danger.

'It wasn't a lie,' Cia retorts.

Ronin takes a menacing step towards us, raises his hand, and almost casually strikes Cia across the back of the head. She goes down without protest. The jar of tadpoles slips from her grasp and shatters on the stony ground. Tiny tadpoles flap feebly around where she lies prone. She must have hit a rock as she fell and blood drips from her nose.

'That's what happens to little girls who *lie*,' he spits.

I am suffused with rage and fear. I make a desperate lunge at him, but he merely sidesteps it, then grabs my arm and twists it up behind my back until I think it must rip from its socket.

'And worse things will happen to little girls who tell any more lies to their mummies.'

He gives my arm one last wrench – I gasp with pain – then steps over Cia's cowering form and is swallowed by the gathering gloom.

'Cia? Cia? Are you okay?'

Cia is weeping softly and spitting blood on to the stones. I can hardly breathe. My stomach knots as I kneel with her in the dirt, wiping the blood from her face. Tears sting my eyes.

That night, when we come in for dinner, we lie to Mom about how Cia sustained her injuries. Ronin sits at the dinner table and watches us closely.

10

Blood and tears and fear. He slakes his need on us. Does Oupa see it? Mom sees only the mask, welded to his face. It is what makes him disturbing.

We spend a lot of time hanging around down by the *khaya* nowadays. The *picanins* squat next to us in the dirt and grin at us. A girl who wears a purple dress with a ruched bodice that's ripped right open squats next to Cia and strokes her arm to see the downy golden hairs bristle. She's plain struck by those hairs – on account of being totally hairless herself. All the *picanins* have just the one clothes hung on them. Our friends are the one with the dirt-coloured school shirt with no buttons, the one with the raggedy pants with the legs rolled up and the pockets falling out the bottom and the one with the grandpa shirt hanging on down to his knees, no pants at all and a crusty nose from the dried snot. The little ones don't wear a stitch of clothing on their bare black hides.

Jobe is there too sometimes. At first Cia acted like it was

her that'd done something wrong – she couldn't look at him. I reckon Jobe could see how bad she felt, because one time he hunkered down next to us and told us that he is an old man who has seen many things and the words of a mere *umfana* did not hurt him. He reckoned he'd even been to jail once and if a man has walked free from a white man's jail there is no end to his luck, and then he told us the story so that Cia'd forget about the business with the washing-machine.

It was after he'd finished working in the gold mines. He headed west and got a job on the railways in a small town just outside Johannesburg. On the main street, which was called 'President Kruger', the music blaring from the juke-boxes in the cafés mingled with the clanging that rose from the railway repair sheds. Also, there was a hotel and a bank and a building society and a cinema. The whites lived in red-brick cottages with rosebushes in the gardens and everything was nice and tidy.

But that was not where Jobe lived. No. Jobe lived in the Location. There were no signs to the Location. To find it, you had to follow the donkey carts and bicycles and women walking with bundles on their heads down past the factories, alongside the fence of the railway yard and across the railway line. And there it was, surrounded by a barbed-wire fence with a gate set on the side furthest away from the town. A dirt track ran alongside the fence through which you could see all the parts of the Location.

First, nearest the railway line, there were thatched wattle huts. They were clumped together behind reed fences where old *makhulus* pounded maize on stone mortars. These were the oldest dwellings and were there even before the fence. Then came a neighbourhood of square cement houses with sheet-iron roofs battened down by rocks. Children played listlessly around the kitchen doors, dogs flopped in the shadow cast by the walls.

Then the neatness ended and the rest was a sprawl of flattened paraffin tins, rusted corrugated iron and flapping sackcloth. Smoke from the night fires hugged it like a blanket in the mornings, turning the sun sallow.

But it wasn't all just sad and ugly. When you got inside, you saw that there were window frames painted bright colours, gates adorned with stolen trellises and patches of flowers, and it hummed with arguments and music, the work of tailors and barbers shaving clients on upturned candle boxes, and flapping enamel signs for Joko Tea and Triumph bicycles. There were shanty churches, and cinemas advertising *High Noon*, women with copper wire coiled around their ankles wearing cheap dresses that were sold at the Indian bazaar, their plaited hair caked with red clay, and men with blankets slung over naked torsos with painted snuff boxes stuck in their pierced lobes. Jobe stayed with his friend Nzimande, but he still had to pay rent because he wasn't a Swazi and the landlady didn't like the look of him.

The Location was ruled by the Location Manager. His name was de la Rey. Jobe had to have his yellow job paper stamped by him. He went to the building and stood in the long line of people that stretched from the desk of de la Rey to the door of the room in which he sat and down the whole length of the *stoep*. Everyone in the line had papers in his hands. There were papers for everything in that place. Pink papers and yellow papers, papers to stay in the Location, papers to leave, papers to get a job, and de la Rey's stamp on your papers was everything. The police roamed the streets like dog-catchers, and if you didn't have the right stamp on your papers you'd be in the back of that van before you even thought of running away.

Not having your pass wasn't the only reason for getting arrested, though. You could get yourself arrested for just about anything – for possessing a spiked stick, for sitting on the wrong bench outside the Court of Native Affairs, for disobedience, trespass, nuisance, impertinence. If things got too quiet in the town, there'd be a raid on the Location and you could get arrested for possessing stolen goods too.

The people came before him one by one. De la Rey almost never looked up. Next. Question. Answer. Bang. Shuffle. But the line never grew shorter. It smelled in there of sweat and insecticide, ink and floor dust.

The people were preparing wonderful celebrations for when he left. Nobody knew when he would go, but they liked to think about him leaving and to plan the celebrations. One man promised to kill four oxen and give a feast to the whole Location. One shebeen queen said she would give free beer for a whole week. There were lots of schemes.

And there were schemes too, to hurry up his leaving. There were ways to make his car have an accident and ways to get a snake to bite him. The schemes went on till late at night. The *sangomas* had serious schemes to give him some sickness. They threw bones and cursed him, but the *tokoloshe* was as scared of him as everybody else.

Then there were the funeral schemes. Who will organize the procession, who will be the pall-bearers, what will the choir sing and on and on. If they ever raised funds for a coffin for de la Rey they'd get enough for a solid gold one.

Jobe shook his head sadly and made clicking sounds with his tongue.

'I don't think he will ever leave.'

Then he went right on discussing the schemes for getting rid of de la Rey.

'The people have strange dreams in that place. They go to the *sangomas* and they say, "Last night I saw the manager in a swarm of bees. What does it mean?"'

The day Jobe went to prison was the day of the riot.

'They were going to make trouble anyway. What kind of trouble I don't know, but I hear them at night in the she-beens talking, talking. Nzimande, he says, "We can count on at least eighty-six in the sheds." I know that Nzimande counted them every day. But I don't think that that trouble was what they planned.'

The trouble started at a public meeting in the square in front of the Location Manager's building. Everybody had to go. First the chief clerk and interpreter told them that all this climbing through the fence up by the train line must stop immediately. Then de la Rey got up and told them about the new law. The new law was that there must be a strip of land at least five hundred yards wide between the

Location and the town it served. In order to comply with the new law, the old quarter would be bulldozed and the fence would be re-erected at the correct distance. It was regrettable but necessary to prevent the evil of *bloed-vermenging* creeping in.

That was what did it. And it was the women who started that trouble.

After de la Rey had told them the new law, the people were angry. They didn't go home like the constables told them. They were shifting there on the square when suddenly one of the women spat at de la Rey.

De la Rey stood there on the *stoep* of the government building. He didn't know what to do. Nothing like that had ever happened in the Location before.

The people were stamping their feet, pounding them hard into the ground in the gathering rhythm of a dance. That was when de la Rey knew to be afraid. He turned and fled into the building.

Jobe chuckled. 'Me, I can still see that old *legotlo* scuttling back into his office that stank of sweat and the ink of his rubber stamp.'

After that the rioters ran through the streets smashing and burning. The fat little *spaza* shop owner who was very rich and drove a Morris Oxford got stabbed in the stomach with a glass bottle. He died on the street in a pool of dark clotted blood.

After a long time, the people stopped being rioters and went home to sit in their hovels and wait for the raid. Everyone knew that there would be a raid. The Location grew very quiet as the night drew on and it waited. Jobe was in his room at Mama Mabaso's when he heard the first sirens.

Finally they came to him. They dragged him out into the street and kicked him in the groin while they ransacked his room. They found his papers and checked for his name on the Lists. He was on the list of Stone Throwers and Clinic Burners, but not on the list of Weapon Brandishers. They threw him into the back of the police van.

In the prison yard, Jobe squatted near the wall.

'We sang "*Vukani, Mzontsundu*" – "Awake, Black Hearts". Then we say, "Africa, *mayibuye*" – "May It Come".'

Afterwards, many weeks later, when it was all over, Jobe had to go back to the Location Manager. His *baas* at the railway job fired him because he was a trouble-maker and he had to get a two-week permit to find work. He stood in the long line outside the office, shuffling forward slowly until at last it was his turn to stand before de la Rey. De la Rey stamped an eviction order instead. He didn't even look up. That was how come Jobe came back to Rhodesia.

Jobe told Cia that after a man has walked free from a white man's prison, he knows he has been blessed by God, and the words of a little boy do not touch him.

After a while the *picanins* go back to playing soccer with a Coke bottle for a ball and they let me and Cia join in, kicking it in the dust. But we can't kick Coke soccer balls for ever. Once it gets dark we have to go home, and whenever we do, there he is, like a spider, waiting. The only thing we get some measure of grim satisfaction from is the escalating hostility between Ronin and Oupa.

*

'Makes for interesting reading, don't you think, Amy?'

'Patrick, I don't think this is the time.'

Mom is warning Oupa. But Oupa doesn't stop. He pulls out a letter and starts reading it right there at the dinner table – when he knows it's against the rules to do anything at the dinner table except eat dinner, and you aren't allowed to do that either while your elbows are on the table or with your fork turned upside-down like a spoon to scoop up peas, and if you talk with your mouth full, you have to leave the dining room altogether and go and eat like a disgusting little pig somewhere else. I stop chewing my chop to watch what Mom will do. Ronin doesn't know how bad it is to read letters or newspapers or anything else at the dinner table and he carries on like nothing's wrong.

'Aunt Amy, if you need anyone to ride out with you tomorrow to check the fences, I can do it. If you need someone?'

'Thank you, Ronin.'

'It must be a record of some sort. Straight Ds,' says Oupa, who doesn't even glance up.

Ronin drops his fork. It clatters on to the floor but he doesn't bend to retrieve it – he's watching Oupa now.

'Patrick. We've already discussed this. It was his first term at a new school and he's been through a lot. His mother . . . Let's not discuss this now.' Her voice is rising. 'Please put that down, Patrick. Sorry, Ronin,' she says to him. 'It's your report from Peterhouse, but we'll talk about it later. Don't worry,' she adds.

'Even managed a D for religious education and PE, for

Chrissake! Thing I'm intrigued about the most is what his housemaster has to say here under "Comments": "Ronin does not seem to have settled in well yet. Let us hope that in the new term his marks improve and that he makes some friends." Probably spend your days getting bog-washed.'

Oupa is chortling. Ronin looks a little ill. His face is still moulded, but something's almost sliding off of it.

Then Oupa sobers up. 'And we're not paying those bloody fees for you to scrape through on your arse, boy!'

'Patrick! That's enough!' Mom says sharply.

After supper Ronin locks himself into his room. Cia and I hear Mom having it out with Oupa in the dining room. She's closed the door, but we dangle through the landing balustrade so we can hear them.

'Patrick, you cannot punish the child for what Seamus and . . .' She trails off.

'You're wrong, Amy. It's treacherous blood that runs in the boy's veins.'

'Oh, for God's sake, Patrick.'

And it doesn't end there. Oupa has enlisted a network of household spies in the war he is waging against Ronin. There's Jobe and Jobe's wife Blessing and Jobe's helpers: Philemon, who does the ironing, and Washington the garden boy. And so while Ronin is as careful as ever to look virtuous around Oupa, behind his back the long-tongued spies whisper in Oupa's ear. As a litany of petty crimes – lies, pilfering and the like – is brought to his attention, Oupa, who is the kind of formidably honest man who has never lied, never cheated in his life, builds his arsenal for righteous persecution. He punishes

Ronin mercilessly. Cia and I bear witness to the punishment, stationed on either side and below Oupa on the judges' bench-*stoep*.

'What is it you hoped to find?'

They are spare words with which to corner a rat.

'Nothing.' Said instinctively, guiltily, followed hastily by 'What do you mean, sir?'

'I was just a-wondering, is all,' Oupa muses, while we wait for him to strike. Ronin, the sun glaring directly in his eyes, squints up at Oupa haloed on the *stoep*. I can't read his expression.

'It's no use, boy. The girlie, Blessing, found it in yer room.' Oupa is gloating odiously now, savouring the moment.

Ronin, sensing he is trapped, shifts nervously.

'Yes, she found your little treasure trove, bundled up neatly under your wardrobe. How do you think letters meant for someone else's eyes – not yours, mind, another's – were hidden way up there?'

The secrets he keeps soon become lies.

'I don't know. I mean, what . . . what letters?' Ronin swallows.

Oupa ignores him. 'I'll tell you what I think. See, I think you stole them, and *that*'s how they found their way there – 'cause you're a sneaky, weaselling little weasel. I seen you sneaking around the place – gives me the creeps. Don't it give you the creeps, lasses?

'Question, though, is why.'

He lingers over the 'why'. Ronin is squirming.

'Maybe you're in love with the owner of them letters, private letters, hmm? Why do you want to know what a man has to say to his wife? Why do you spy on them?'

Ronin never utters a word. He knows what Oupa is hinting at, although we do not, and dares not say anything.

'Me brother would die of shame, you know.' Then he twists the dagger he's plunged between Ronin's flinched shoulder-blades. 'I'll have to tell Amy, of course – she'll have been missing what's hers.'

Ronin looks anguished. 'Please, sir,' I can see it costs him dearly to beg, 'please, sir, don't tell her. Please.'

Hunted eyes look up at me. Still, there is a paucity of pity for him in my heart. And in the background there is the persistent nasal rasping of Oupa's disapproval.

He seems to draw on a bottomless vat of bitterness in his often unprovoked attacks on Ronin. It tastes like tannin on my tongue. Something deep inside Oupa is corroded, and the corrosion seeps out, contaminating the air around us. He makes us complicit in his sniping too – he needs us to keep score, to be on his side. It makes me feel used. The bitterness comes from Oupa's past, maybe from his brother's stolen freedom – a salve for the chafing.

In the end, his persecution of Ronin makes me uneasy. I sit and see what Oupa can't or won't beneath the penitence. With each trial Ronin's hooded eyes glower more. I know it doesn't bode well for us, and we are bound to silence.

11

'*Eina!*'
Cia has twisted her ankle on a fallen branch sunk into the mulch.

'*Ssssh*, man! You'll wake him,' I hiss. We are close to his tree.

'Sorry, Nyree.'

I can barely see her in the gloom as she limps a little way behind me. It's late in the night and even darker on the forest floor where no starlight ever reaches. My fingertips tingle with fright, but I stumble on through the labyrinth of roots. We have no choice, we need to make the offering.

I feel the eyes of the fairies on me with every footfall and there are pinpricks of magic in the air. I am thankful now that we made our escape – the night is full of promise. Once again we were almost caught, this time by Ronin. We opened the door to our room a chink and searched the passage for light. Finding none, we crept out towards the landing. Half-way there, though, the door to Ronin's room opened behind us with a creak. We froze, both too stupid with fright to hide. Somehow being caught by him in the darkness seemed terrifying. Everything stayed dark, he never turned on the light, but I could sense him in the doorway, his eyes trying to probe the shadows. He couldn't – it was very late and the blackness in Modjadji's long, windowless corridors had become total. After an age we heard his door creak slowly shut, heard his bed groan behind it, and we fled downstairs, out through the window and into the forest that rose behind Modjadji.

Our exhilaration was soon extinguished as we entered the woods. Magic is a dangerous thing and it sobers you up like a slap in the face.

As my fingers grope around the gnarly bark of a tree-trunk, I wonder if we'll see any fairies tonight. I'm half hoping we will, half hoping we won't. Fairies are strange beings. They dine on the perfume of flowers; toadstools spring where fairy feet have gone and they cast a white shadow. There are fairies of the earth and of the air, and water fairies, who dwell in lakes, rivers, pools, springs, wells, fountains and even in raindrops and tears. There are pixies and pooks and a little hobgoblin called Boon, who protects children from bad dreams, and a fairy dies every time someone says they don't believe in them.

But not all fairies are good. There are bad fairies too. Bad fairies' power is drawn from the dark side of the moon. Like Water Fay. She lives at the reed-choked edges of lonely ponds. She lures you with her song and her eyes, which are like fragments of the earth's soul. Her hands caress you and

114

pull you down into her watery embrace. And there you will lie for ever, your eyes unseeing, weeds clogging your mouth.

We have come to pay homage to one of the dark fairies. I spy his tree just ahead and something grips my innards.

'Cia. There it is.' I point at the tree that, even in the gloom, stands stark.

Cia is afraid. It will give us away. 'Go on,' she whispers.

The Darkling is his name. He is nestled somewhere in the tree's grey roots, but his nostrils prickle in the fear-tinged air. His eyelids flutter. His hollow belly growls. He licks the darkness, smells fear on his tongue. I am also afraid. Cia and I know only too well that it is unwise to follow the path to the place where this fairy slumbers, that only St John's wort and the peal of church bells can ward him off. But tonight – tonight we seek him out. We are the first in a long time. The Darkling is forgotten. No one remembers the soul-plunderer, no one feeds him to protect themselves any more. The old souls in his guts have gone sour and they howl with hunger. Oh, how he longs to place his parched lips over another's and suck out the *umoya*, slick with moans. He unfurls from the dead tree, to which spring will never come again, and claws at the bark which had begun to grow on him.

I cannot see him, but I know he is crouching in the roots, waiting.

'Okay, Nyree, give it to him,' Cia whispers urgently.

I kneel and place our offering under the tree. Cia kneels beside me. The scarab lies on a bed of rotting leaves. It's really just the husk of a dead rhino beetle we found, but it looks like Cia's and I'm hoping the Darkling won't notice.

115

Then I push the candle into a little mound of earth in front of it and try to strike a Lion match, but I am trembling and a pile of splinters grows under my hands. At last I light one and touch the flame to the wick of the candle. It flickers eerily.

'O Darkling, please take this offering and don't let him steal our mom from us. Thank you.'

'Ah men,' says Cia.

I've said what we have to say. I don't have any more words. 'Okay, let's go.'

'Do you think it'll work?' Cia whispers anxiously, as she gets up off her knees.

I don't answer her. 'Come on. Hurry. Let's get away from here.'

The Darkling blinks slowly behind me.

12

It is late in the summer, and our watcher has to go back to school. He has a hangdog look about him, but I don't feel sorry for him, no siree, and as he is driven morosely out of the front gates, my spirits soar.

'I hope they chain him up in the basement for the whole term,' says Cia, beside me on the *stoep*, with feeling.

'*Ja*, me too – in the pitch dark with no food or water until he's starving to death.'

'*Ja!* And – and bubonic-plague rats gnawing on him.'

'And he's just *begging* to be let out.'

'I hope – I hope he gets the bubonic plague himself and is covered in boils!' Cia throws in, breathless at our sadism.

She gives me a Chinese bangle, and we stand there long after the noise of the engine has grown faint, her wringing the skin on my wrists, feeling pleased. The slackening of the house's tendons is almost palpable, as though we were all condemned men – dead men walking – who've been granted a pardon. Cia and I don't have to go back to school for another two weeks, and I gulp down lungfuls of free-dom.

We slip to the languor of high summer. We spend the days crocodiling through the waterhole that Dad built for us on one of the lower terraces above the farmhouse, slathering, half submerged, over hairy mangoes, basking like bloated hippos on the rocks, and then, when the sun begins to boil us from the inside, peeling ourselves off with a satisfying slurp from the suction, and flopping back into the tepid water. Once it has revived us, we dive and tor-pedo our way through the watery lapis-lazuli, the sunlight undulating through fronds of furry green algae.

Few things disrupt our sun-steeped drunkenness. Cia gets stung by a wasp after she sticks her mouth over a pipe jutting out above the edge of the waterhole and I get a putsi-fly larvae boil in my back, which has to be smeared in Vaseline to suffocate it. I'm not allowed in the water for days on end while Oupa waits for it to come up for air so he can squeeze it out. One afternoon, when Cia and I are kneeling on Mom's little dressing-table stool rummaging in her drawer, sticking tortoiseshell combs in our hair and wrapping strings of pol-ished tiger's eye and rose-quartz beads around our necks, we find a letter from Ronin specially written to her. It says, 'Dear Amy,' on it, no one else. He says he's fine but he hopes she'll write to him and that he thinks about her often. Cia tears it up. I'm worried that Mom will miss it, but there's nothing we can do now. Other than that, time drifts on a gentle current, until the anticipation of another road trip begins to eddy and swirl around us.

On the day of the road trip we're loaded with Oupa into the back of the old Peugeot station-wagon sporting orange fur on the dashboard. Mom and Dad, who's back home from call-up, are in the front, and we set forth for the convoy rendezvous. It is, of course, by far the greatest way to travel cross-country – like being in a parade, a military parade, with a regulatory rifle propped up out of every driver's window. At the rendezvous we enlist with the motley collection of cars sporting bumper stickers that read, 'Don't Drive Rhodesia Dry', 'Rhodesia is Super' and 'Chipangali Wildlife Orphanage', hundreds of people, dogs, guns, a caterwauling of noise and *ousies* wandering up and down the long line selling trays of *koeksusters*, which the Afrikaner women make.

Cia and I stand at the side of the road propped up against each other at the shoulder under an acacia tree, shaded from the syrupy heat, dripping juice from our *koeksusters*, staring at the armoured personnel carriers. There are three – one to ride front, middle and back of the convoy that won't drive Rhodesia dry and thinks Rhodesia is Super. They're dressed in camouflage to match the soldiers poking up out of the top hatches of the great swivelling gun turrets. Dell reckons one of those'd turn a Terr to roadkill in a second. Then he makes *rut-tut-tut* noises and jerks spasmodically as he empties the magazine of his imaginary mounted gun in a wide arc, turning Terrs to roadkill in seconds. Cia rolls her eyes. Right now *miggies* are swarming in a *miggie* mask around Cia's face and she's snorting and spitting to disperse them. Rivulets of syrup trickle down my chin.

The graze doesn't end with the *koeksusters* either. Back in the car, slicked to the seat, even though we already have a whole coolbox of *padkos*, we are still allowed to guzzle bottles of cream soda and frozen penny cools and chocolate Fredo Frogs at every jacaranda- and flame-tree-lined town from Gatooma to Que Que to Gwelo until my stomach queases, and Cia's queases so bad she reckons she's gonna honk and our eyes are sugared glitter balls. We get into a feverish slapping fight for crossing the invisible line down the seat between us, but if we don't stop it this instant Mom's going to throw us both out and drive off, leaving us to fend for ourselves in the wild. Oupa reckons it's doubtful we'd last one night, being the gormless nitwits we are. We buy a red and black lucky-bean necklace each from roadside *picanins* and hang out the window and sing, 'This land is your land, this land is my land.'

'If they should tell you that you should leave it, don't you believe it, it isn't true,' Cia sings, off-key, at the top of her lungs, but the wind whips her voice away into nowhere as the endless woodland savannah flashes by.

We spend the night outside Que Que at a motel of khaki-green, thatched rondavels adorned with florid curtains and bedspreads. We wallow in the deep enamel bath and order egg mayonnaise and tinned fruit salad in syrup for dinner from the dining room's à-la-carte menu.

When we arrive at our destination, the Victoria Falls Hotel, its deceptively derelict, bullet-riddled façade opening into a plush velvet-curtained interior, Cia and I are overawed. It is set in the gardens of Babylon, which merge with the rainforest fringing the falls, the mist plume arching over the lawns. Tea is served on the veranda by waiters in starched linen uniforms. Every table gets a stack of silver trays with sandwiches on the bottom, scones on the next tray and tiny iced cake squares on the smallest one at the very top. Mom says it is a relic from a bygone era. As we leopard-crawl up the banisters of the great sweeping staircases, I inhale the musty ghosts from times past that float down from the eaves like dust. From under the tables in the Livingstone Room, laden with ageing linen, silver and crystal, I can still hear the echo of balls held long ago.

'Can you hear them, Cia?'

'*Ssssh!*'

'What?'

'I don't want them to hear us, okay?'

We are here because Dad's going to be on television. He has joined the Rhodesian Action Party, because the Rhodesian Action Party knows that Smithy is going to sell us out. It is only a matter of time. It's very important that the Rhodesian Action Party warns people. Oupa says it's already too late, any ruddy arse can see that. And we must be deaf as well as blind if we can't hear the strains of the infernal savages' victory dance in the night – he's not ashamed to admit that he lies there cowering in his bed, listening to the pounding of drums and the slap of bare feet in the dirt – and he'll warrant the infernal savages are sharpening their *pangas* for a spot of *murungu* blood-letting as we speak. His nerves are destroyed and he has to have an extra G and T of an afternoon for them.

Still, Oupa says, it's fitting that our father is here fighting for Rhodesia at the last, since our own forebear's blood was spilled at its birth. Oupa is always going on about how Cia's and my pedigree goes all the way back to the founding of Rhodesia. It was our grandmother's mother, he says, who had to fight the bloodthirsty savages to save Rhodesia for the Queen. Erin was her name, and Oupa expects me and Cia to live up to Erin's grit. Erin and her family were settlers who came with the pioneers to start Rhodesia. They were settled good and nicely in Rhodesia, but then there was the war.

When the war came, the people of the Mashonaland fought side by side with their old enemy, the people of the Matabele, like brothers. It was because of a dream by the great and powerful *n'anga*, Ambuya Nehanda. By the light of a fire, Jobe told us that these were the words of she whose spirit comes from the beginning of time: 'Listen to the voices of the dead. Spread yourselves like darkness across the land at night and fight until the stranger leaves. There is only this time now, and we must fight.'

'Who were the strangers, Jobe, who were they?'

'You, little one, it was you, the *abelungu*. The people, they wanted their freedom in their land, the land of their birth and of their ancestors.'

'Oh.' Silence. 'Well, we're not leaving, Jobe – are we, Nyree?' Cia said defiantly and then, as an afterthought, 'Can't we all live here, Jobe?'

Jobe reckons that loads of the Afs are already squabbling over who gets the land after all the white people are dead

122

and they've gone and put curses on the double-crossing neighbours who're trying to steal their bit. I said, 'Why will all the white people be dead?' Jobe said he didn't know.

Oupa says that Erin was stranded with her family on their remote farm with hordes of murderous savages between them and the Bulawayo laager, and Cia and I can get down on our two knees every night and thank God that they survived the harrowing flight to the safety of the laager or we wouldn't be here to tell the tale. Cia and I can also get down on our two knees every night and thank God that we weren't born *munts* or Saxon.

At the bottom of the veranda steps there are white-linen-draped tables set out under great spreading mango trees, their heavy skirts fluttering demurely in the breeze, with a bank of cameras mounted on tripod contraptions aimed at them. We're going to be allowed to stay up extra late to watch the *Eight o'Clock News* on TV.

In the meantime we prance through the mists of the rainforest by the falls like forest sprites, swim in the Roman bath-pool, then let our sylphlike selves down by dancing wildly, thrashing about and kicking to the primitive beat of the African drums that pulse through the night for the benefit of the few fascinating foreigners who've dared to trespass in this wondrous, forsaken land. That night Cia falls asleep curled up in a stiff, leather-backed chair in the hotel lounge before the *Eight o'Clock News* and misses seeing Dad in black and white on the edge of the white linen-draped table warning everybody before it is too late.

Afterwards we visit the strange moonscape of the Matopos, made of humpback granite domes, adorned with uncanny balancing rock formations and strewn with giant's marbles where a stack has toppled. On the summit of Malindidzimu, the savannah spreading out below us, we pose self-consciously for a photograph at Rhodes's grave, Cia trying to smile prettily at the camera, unwittingly doing her most indelible impression of a wickedly smug little Chinese simian.

On the way home, Cia and I are fighting a bitter, silent battle on our side of the back seat. I deliberately extend my arm across the line, my index finger protruding out of my balled fist. I am trespassing now. Cia watches the advance impassively. Then I poke my finger into her thigh, the tip probing deeply into her soft flesh.

'Mom, she *touched* me!' Cia retorts victoriously.

At that point something ruptures in the Peugeot's engine. We hear an ominous muffled explosion and smoke spews out from under the bonnet. She shudders and limps to the verge before dying, gasping for air.

We squat in the stillness at the side of the road on the exposed roots of an old baobab tree, listening to the silence rent by the high-pitched whine of the cicadas, awaiting Dad's return. He's run to the nearest village to get help, but since it is a few miles away, he won't be back before nightfall. As the shadows lengthen, Mom makes us get back into the car and won't let us out, not even when Cia has to go – instead she has to roll down the window, stick her bottom out of it and wee suspended in mid-air, her wee streaking down the side of the dead Peugeot. I giggle rudely.

Then the mood changes. The slack, cicada-wrung lethargy of the day is plucked taut. Mom is tense, straining. Fear lies rolled up on the floor between us, like a damp, snotty piece of toilet paper, unacknowledged. Nobody wants to say it. *Terrs*. But they're out there. Oupa props the rifle between his knees.

The stories flit silently around the car. Attacks on lonely roads, mothers bayoneted to their children as they tried to protect them with their bodies, men gunned down as they knelt in supplication. In the twilight we sit and wait for them to find us. Me and Cia stop fighting. I feel like I've been wired to something.

Suddenly there is a disturbance in the bush near by. All breathing stops as we strain to hear. There is a rustling noise and something small and furry shoots out of the undergrowth and hurtles towards the car. It launches itself from several metres off and thumps against the window. Cia yelps, either with fright or pain, as Mom yanks the two of us into her protective custody. Momentary silence ensues after the stunned creature has slid to the ground, but it's not long before it has shaken itself and relaunched itself at the window. After a second jarring collision, it takes to bouncing up and down, trying to see through the glass. Curiosity overcomes Cia and me and we wriggle free of Mom's grasp, lean over and peer at the flapping ears outside.

'It's a puppy!' yells Cia.

After this proclamation we watch our interloper for a minute longer, before Cia reaches the inescapable conclusion that 'He wants to come in, Mom! Mom, please can we let him in?'

Oupa refuses point-blank. Mom backs him up. Neither Cia nor I nor the dog is deterred. It keeps begging us, and we keep begging Mom, to no avail. In the end, though, our intercession isn't necessary. When the dog, exhausted, takes to lying by the car, crying pitifully to himself, Mom can take it no more. She relents and climbs into the back of the station-wagon to open it. Oupa calls her a bleeding-hearted sap.

Even as the handle turns the dog, sensing his chance, springs to attention. The hatch has barely been opened a crack when he vaults joyously inside and throws himself on to his rescuers in a frenzy of licking gratitude. This is where Mom draws the line. Holding him firmly she tells him that that is enough, and that it's not as though he gave us any choice in the matter.

Afterwards Mom looks even sorrier that she didn't draw the line sooner. He is small, a terrier of dubious pedigree, mangy, flea-bitten and emaciated. We give him the leftover chicken drumsticks from our somewhat depleted *padkos* cache, which he wolfs without waiting for us to unwrap all of the tinfoil.

After he's eaten our remaining two packets of Willards crisps and half a cheese and jam sandwich, we sit surveying each other. There is a quiet tap-tap at the window. We shriek, including Oupa and the dog. In the gathering gloom, Dad's face looms at the window. He's got the part he needs.

Even while Dad and Oupa grapple with the engine by weak torchlight, Mom's relief that the waiting and watching and hair-on-end apprehension are over is transmitted to us. In the aftermath, it is rather festive in the back of the car, albeit tinged with hysteria. At the dog's adoption, Dad merely shakes his head. And when we are finally on our way, he shakes it again when we are obliged to admit that a certain waif and stray has eaten the last of the chicken drumsticks he'd ordered. The waif in question curls up into the smallest ball possible between Cia and me and goes to sleep.

13

His name is Moosejaw. Oupa reckons he ought to be christened Tuckshop, since it's painfully obvious that he's naught but a *kaffir* terrier. Then he sniggers. But Moosejaw suits him better. In any event, Moosejaw doesn't care. His devotion to Cia and me is the same whatever we name him.

None of the other dogs in the farm pack is as devoted to us. Certainly none is prepared to suffer the indignity of flushing out fairies in the forest while sporting a tiara. Moosejaw ate Cia's *shongololo* once during the heats and got bawled out by her for getting her disqualified and then he foamed *shongololo* at the mouth. He was deeply remorseful afterwards: he slunk about for the rest of the day with his tail curled up under his belly. Now he just watches as the *shongololos* in their black armour-plating surf past his salivating jaws on waves of undulating legs.

Vumba, Smiler and Digby, the three musketeering Alsatians, got bored of us years ago. Now Digby stares balefully at us when we try to garnish his hairy Alsatian muzzle with a sequined bridal veil from the dress-up box, then yawns and stalks off in disgust, his sidekicks, Vumba and Smiler, in tow.

Moosejaw can exercise military self-discipline in the face of almost any distraction. Not for him the joys of hunting and herding. Even when the musketeers hare off after a flock of guinea fowl, Moosejaw remains stoically at our side, only a quiver of yearning muscle in his haunches betraying the toll it takes on him. Moosejaw's devotion costs him dearly in pack rank, though.

In the beginning, Vumba, Smiler and Digby fought Moosejaw every day with fresh gusto. Digby'd saunter past Moosejaw, like he was minding his own business. Then, without warning, he'd turn and pounce with a bloodcurdling howl, the cue for the others to join in. Moosejaw mooched around sporting gashed flanks and tattered ears. But after a while, his cringing got to them and they left him alone. Now they pretend he isn't there, which, as a pitiful foster-dog, is the best he can hope for. Luckily Moosejaw's loyalty lies not with canine but with human members of his surrogate family. And so he has whittled for himself his own place in our household, his only peculiarity coming out at mealtimes.

Moosejaw can detect the dull, tinny noise of the enamel dog bowls being taken off the kitchen shelves from miles off. At the sound, he instantly abandons whatever we're doing and bolts towards the kitchen as though the Cloven-hoofed One himself were after him, Oupa says. While Jobe decants *sadza* and gristly stew into the assembled bowls on the counter, Moosejaw crouches at his feet, poised to pounce, fixated on the preparations continuing above. Within minutes, though, he loses faith and patience and starts whining in agitation. Eventually, out of sheer desperation, he resorts to frenzied leaping at the counter. By the time Jobe has called the others in to dinner, he's a shuddering, drooling wreck.

When he finally gets his food, he wolfs it with rabid savagery, choking down huge mouthfuls, then tries to plunder from the others, of which they take a very dim view. Since Moosejaw won't, or can't, be daunted by the deep growling and fang-baring of dogs twice his size, every mealtime ends in a hullabaloo of gnashing teeth and flying fur.

At first we thought his voracious appetite would subside with time, but long after starvation should have retreated to a distant memory, Moosejaw continues to behave as though every meal is his last. The spectre of hunger never ceases to haunt him. Eventually we take to impounding him at mealtimes. He is put in the laundry room to eat his meals alone and is only permitted out once everyone else has had enough time to demolish theirs. Even then he pounces on the empty dog bowls and absconds with them to his kennel if they aren't stowed away beforehand.

Once he got up on the kitchen table where the basin of offal stood, and by the time Jobe came back, Moosejaw had eaten his way through a mountain of gizzards, tongue and tripe and was lying on his side in the middle of the entrails feast, his distended belly literally threatening to burst, still eating. Oupa called him a gluttonous vulture and recommended that we leave him to gorge himself to death.

Fairy flushing might not be where Moosejaw's usefulness ends either. He might also be the way into the attic where Angélique's belongings are stored. Cia and I never knew our grandmother – she died when our father was only a small boy – so an aura of mystique hangs about her.

She was bitten by a snake. It doesn't say so on her grave, but Jobe told us that that was how she died. We went down there with Moosejaw, to the graveyard, just after he came to live with us. There's a whitewashed chain strung from stone corner stakes that you have to climb over to get in. Then we inspected each of the gravestones. There are four. Moosejaw inspected them with us; he sniffed them, scratched the dirt beneath each one and wagged his tail to and fro. Angélique's says 'Beloved wife and mother' on it. Jobe says it was a mamba that bit her and even me and Cia know what getting bitten by a mamba means. Jobe once saw a herd boy get bitten by one. The herd boy was walking in the bush when the snake struck him. Jobe saw the glint of the sun on its back as it slithered away. He ran up to the herd boy, who had fallen to the ground, but there was nothing he could do. Everybody in the Vumba knows there isn't much you can do about death.

Jobe's heard tell it was her hand that was bitten, Angélique's. They say the hand is the worst place for a snake bite, that's what they say. If a mamba bites you on the hand, you're dead before you hit the ground. For a bite from a boomslang, a rinkhals or a puff adder, a rat's-claw scratch will nearly always work. But when a man is bitten by a mamba, that's it. Then it is God's will that a prayer be said over his grave before the hole in the veld is covered over with the dark earth.

Oupa has never told us any of this, but one time he said, '*Munts*? I can tell you a thing or two about *munts*. They are the scourge of Africa. The righteous might fear the Almighty and stand in awe of His creation, but even they must wonder why He made the *munt* and the black mamba.'

That is how we know it is true. Then he mumbled about the indolence of *munts*, which is one of the low points of their character, along with thievery, and about the fact that if you wanted a job done properly, you had to do it yourself. Although there were some good *munts*, who did do the job properly and who didn't steal your tools, and he always thought that it wasn't right to kill that kind of *munt*.

Once Oupa told us about the time he saw a snake-charmer turn his staff into a serpent. It was in the old Transvaal a long time ago. Oupa was travelling to Johannesburg to buy a new Ford Model A. He was staying overnight in Potgietersrus and couldn't resist the attraction of the Saturday night *skou* in the old town hall. First there was a speech by the man from the Volkskas, then the *predikant* said a prayer. After the prayer, there was the prophet Oom Schalk van Niekerk who could foretell that a drought was coming. Then the Potgietersrus schoolmaster did a poetry recital. But the poem didn't even rhyme and the Potgietersrus district *boers* booed him off the stage and the schoolmaster called them a bunch of soulless Philistines and said they knew as much about art as boomslangs and then afterwards there was a debate about the native question, which was always a popular subject, but nobody wanted to do the question about whether the native women in the Locations should have to carry passes, which was too hard, and one of the old *boers* said they should just be allowed to talk about how the *kaffirs* in the Potgietersrus district were getting cheekier every day. Then there was a dance and the *boere orkes* played lively dance tunes like '*Sarie Marais*' and '*Vat Jou Goed en Trek, Ferreira*'* and Oupa could *lang-arm* with the best of those *boers*, but it was the Muslim who turned the rod into a snake that left Oupa cold.

'Like Moses before Pharaoh, the Muslim cast down that rod and it became a serpent. I tell you, lasses, there was no trickery, no trickery that I could discern, but little did I know that the shiver down my spine was a foreboding of the evil that the serpent would bring me in this life.'

He has never come as close to telling us how Angélique died. It's maybe why we like to go back to the cemetery: her death, Great-grandfather's, all our ancestors', are secrets we can almost touch there.

Anyhow, we went there with Moosejaw, who was scratching and sniffing keenly when a queer thing happened. Cia bent over Angélique's grave, as if she was going to trace the inscription on the gravestone, and as she did so, there was a rustle in the grass at her feet, a quiver of blade, but before I could see what it was, Moosejaw had pounced on it. He leaped and a snake coiled right up into the air and landed with a thud a short way off. Before it could even wind into

*'Get Your Stuff and Go, Ferreira' (Afrikaans)

the long grass, Moosejaw had seized it between his jaws and chomped right through its neck. Then he sat there with the broken mamba at his feet, right pleased with himself. Cia looked at me and then at Moosejaw, then stared fixedly at the dead snake.

'*Jeez*, Moosejaw, thanks.'

There was a slight sheen on her brow. I thought how strange it was that a mamba had chosen to live by Angélique's grave. Ever since that day, though, the temptation to find what she left behind has grown in me like a thirst.

It's like Moosejaw was meant to help us.

I tell Cia that, with Moosejaw on guard, there's no way that Oupa will catch us, no way José.

'But we're not *allowed*, Nyree.'

I tell her that she's a big scaredy-cat and that me and Moosejaw are going to do it without her. Finally she succumbs. 'I did pray to the Lor' Jesus to make me good, Nyree, but the Lor' Jesus didn't.'

It is late afternoon. Oupa is snoring in his wicker throne, his snores rhythmically stretching and slackening his braces over his bulging belly. His false teeth grin in the ice-cube melt at the bottom of his gin glass. The air is drunk and lazy. Fat lizards idle in a stupor next to the enthroned Oupa on the *stoep*, their bulbous, blue-green scales gleaming lizardly. Wasps wasp noisily in the gauze across the front-door screen. A glutinous bubble of spittle bursts in the corner of Oupa's sagging mouth. At the end of the long dark corridor on the second floor Cia and I sneak up the steep, rickety wooden stairs that lead to the attic.

135

Our stealth is sufficient for Moosejaw to grasp the need for wariness – he mounts the stairs like a predator stalking prey, pausing to listen intently before placing each paw warily on the next step. I open the heavy oak door and creep inside. Cia, with the mange-ridden Grover in tow, follows. Moosejaw brings up the rear and stations himself close to the doorway.

The secrecy, the whispering, the illicit thrill of the forbidden charge the attic air with static. Muted, dust-flecked light streams through the tiny window, gently illuminating old cheval mirrors and armoires, draped bassinets and other fading antique glories. Fleshy geckos watch, bemused, from dim stone walls, billowing with shadows and the mouldy breath of ancestors. As soon as my eyes have grown accustomed to the semi-gloom, they rove about the room until I see them, Angélique's trunks, stacked against the far wall. There are three, great wooden tea chests, lined up next to an old cast-iron Singer treadle sewing-machine.

'There, Cia, that's them!' I whisper theatrically.

Angélique was born on a mission station on the shores of Lake Nyasa to an Afrikaans missionary by the name of Jan Christiaan de Beer. He took the name from the very first Christiaan de Beer who came to Africa. Oupa says that our great-grandfather, Jan Christiaan, was a puritan who wielded a Bible in one hand and a *sjambok* in the other.

'She could recite her father's great trials by rote, my Angélique. She feared him, you know, lasses. After he was ordained, Jan Christiaan took his Bible and ventured forth into the ungodly wilderness of Africa. He crossed the track-less thirstlands of the Kalahari to reach the fermenting jungles of the great floodplains whereupon he was struck down with fever. At the confluence of the Chobe and the Zambezi, he languished for days in a savage's hut. But God had not forsaken him, and when he awoke and beheld the pagan tribeswomen of the Makololo, wantonly parading their nakedness, he covered his eyes from their shame and warned them that the emissaries of the Lord would smite the sinners who came heedless of their nakedness into His sight. Woe unto them!

'He healed the sick. In the waters of the Kwando, the Linyati, the Kavango rivers he baptized the saved, and after, with the light of Jesus Christ shining down upon their labour, he watched as they felled jungle trees to raise high the cross above the mission church.

'In the laager at Bulawayo, where he found himself shel-tered while the dark tribes of Ham were amassing in the unholy wilderness beyond where the blessed light of Jesus shone not, he came across a young convert in your great-grandmother, Erin.'

The tribes of Ham are the *munts* because God condemned them to slavery for ever amen, which doesn't seem fair to Cia and me, seeing as all Ham did was snigger when his father Noah – who begat Ham – got drunk and lolled around buck naked. It was after God was finished drowning all the sinners and everybody'd got off the ark that it happened. And if it weren't for the goody-goody brothers who snitched on Ham, Noah wouldn't ever even have known.

'He promised her teeming swamps where the lost souls wallowed in sin, crying out for the word of God, and she accepted his hand in marriage.'

So after she was done doing her duty and fighting the bloodthirsty hordes to save Rhodesia for the Queen, Erin went and married Jan Christiaan, which was a disgrace to her kin, seeing as he was an Afrikaner.

Cia and I aren't surprised. Dutchmen, also called bone-heads, are slow-witted. They roll their Rs around on their tongues when they speak and they have bonehead names like Koos and Kristoffel, which is how come Koos and Kristoffel get jeered at behind the bicycle sheds at school and get stuck in the thickos class, and they have seascape paintings in their *voorkamers* with waves crested by galloping white horse heads and doilies on their dining-room tables, which just shows you what bog-trotting yokels they are.

Cia and I reckon that old Jan Christiaan would turn in his grave if he knew that his grandson, Dad, had fought in Afrikaner versus English battles on the battleground of primary school on the side of the English. At first break Dad says that both sides were forced to sit at their desks and drink their quarts of milk, which the teacher doled out. It smelled foul and he gagged when he swallowed it, but at least it pumped up his strength ready for the second break clay-lekky fights behind the bicycle sheds. Dad and his gang flung at the boneheads clay missiles from twig catapults, which inflict grievous bodily harm, although we have this only second hand since Dad bust us making mud cannon-balls for our own clay-lekky battle and gave us a hiding.

But Oupa says Jan Christiaan also got banished from his *volk* and *vaderland* to the mission station in Nyasaland far to the north on account of marrying Erin, who was English. She died giving birth to her seventh and last child, Angélique.

Sometimes, on wobbling-jowl days, Oupa remembers something of Angélique aloud: 'Aye, she was a beautiful lass, my Angélique. Long dark hair that shone like burnished copper in the sunlight.'

Like mine.

Without a mother, Angélique was nursed instead by big-bosomed African women.

'Her first language, she told me, was Chinyanga, the language of the Lake, although later she learned to speak both Afrikaans and English and the language of fear.

'There is naught so villainous a character in all of fiction, lasses, as the God of the Old Testament. A vain, petty, cruel bully with a lust for bloodshed and, by all accounts, your great-grandfather was his most devoted disciple.'

His stories of how, mired among the sinners of the flesh, her father was goaded into violence, of how Angélique fled when she was but sixteen, of how, when he wed her, her father disowned her, make me hanker for her possessions in those chests. I want to stroke them. I want to be near to her.

Just after they were married Oupa went back once with her to the mission station. Cia wanted to know if there were palm trees and young converts in flimsy white nightgowns getting baptized in the water like in Babylon. But Oupa said, no, he did not recall palm fronds or white-muslin-clad

139

converts. He recalled the stink, the filth, the innumerable feral children with snotty noses and oozing, red-rimmed eyes, and scabs that they constantly picked and ate. There was a hospital. Blood. Pus. Shit. The church. Beggars begging God. Old Jan Christiaan said if Angélique wished to bind herself to a disciple of idolatrous Jesuits she was no daughter of his. They left, never to return.

Mom has told us, though, that when he married Angélique, Oupa too suffered at his own father's hand for his marriage to a Protestant, though Oupa will never admit to it. And then Angélique died, like her mother before her, leaving Oupa to raise his son alone.

We cross the room, our footsteps leaving a trail of small footprints in the dust. I kneel in front of the chests stamped 'Produce of Empire: These are the Sinews of War' and plastered with peeling posters emblazoned with the shipping insignia of the White Star Line, afraid that they will be locked. Thankfully they aren't. The first of the three opens grudgingly when I lift the latch and we heave on the rasping, rusty-hinged lid. It opens to us another world – a romantic, lavender-potpourried world lost for ever to time.

Angélique's private trousseau of delicate lace and linen is shrouded in tissue paper, along with the accoutrements of a coming-out in society – her dainty silver dance-card-holder, black filigree fans, silk gloves, ornate lipstick-holders and snuff boxes and her dressing-table toilette – exquisite perfume bottles with little vaporizing pumps, silver and ivory mirror-and-comb sets and old-fashioned jars of Pond's cold cream, the faded labels, promising the elixir of youth, curling at the edges. Draped in mink stoles and dripping in clip-on earrings, we are in heaven.

Inside the last trunk we find a leatherbound water-stained diary. I haul it out and as I do so, a sliver of photos slips on to the floor. Sepia ghosts from a lost world on a lake in central Africa stare out at us. There is a picture of Oupa as a dashing young soldier in the Allied Army destined for the deserts of North Africa, and there is even one of his brother, Seamus. Angélique has written his name on the back, although it's hard to decipher her florid handwriting. In the picture he's grinning self-consciously, his hair sticking up at the back of his head, not knowing that he's going to die real soon, shot in a skirmish with a *kaffir*. Curiously, in his arms he cradles a tiny baby.

'Cia, do you think this is *his* baby, Seamus's? If it is, it must be Ronin's mother!'

We've intruded on something intimate, secret. But we keep riffling, greedily, guiltily. The ghosts of our ancestors crowd around – they whisper together in dry, crêpey whispers from the corners of the attic. I can smell their breath, and smells, like music, hold memories.

14

With the passing of time comes the ending of summer, and cold, brittle winds whip round the keen edges of the mountain and down into the gullies. Old Modjadji feels more lonely and isolated, as though the wind is severing something warm and fuggy. It's also dry, drier even than usual for the season. The rains have been poor this year; they petered out before the second half of our summer rains even began, and time is almost up before the long, dry winter sets in irreversibly. Drought is loitering in the shadows.

Oupa says drought is Africa's nemesis. Every few years, the nemesis descends, the rains fail, the skin of the earth is burned by the pitiless sun till it splits, and we are left gasping until it chooses to relent. Fear of the nemesis is infectious, something that's airborne, which you breathe into your lungs. As it lands its claws puncture the heart, and from then on it lives in you. Its velvety dorsal tufts throb gently, and you search the skies anxiously every year from October and try to interpret the omens that forecast the rains. This year the omens predicted good rains. They always do.

Our forest floor is carpeted with furled brown leaves that crunch underfoot. Normally they melt into mulch in the damp, but the desiccated air just turns them to tinder. Then our lush undergrowth, parched and sapless, dies slowly of thirst. The stream that usually tumbles down the mountainside dries up and we find the shrivelled little carcasses of frogs who tarried too long to hibernate. Still the rains don't come. Sometimes great swollen and bruised cumulo-nimbus clouds roil off the distant crags to taunt us, but in the end the wind rails against them, making them hoard their watery load until they disintegrate to nothing.

One evening as Cia and I are leaving our naked forest glade, the veil of ivy that once clothed it having long ago withered away, Cia pauses to grind a shrivelled fern frond to dust between her fingers. She watches the powder float downwards, then looks up at me and says, 'It's like some of the magic is gone, Nyree. Like it's dying softly.'

I look back at her. She's bathed in a shaft of light, leaves streaming around her. I say nothing.

With the heel of her Bata *takkie*, Cia rolls back an old husk of a log. We like to roll back old rotted logs in the forest – it's one of our rituals, normally a gratifying one: tiny rootlets and fungus spittle pull apart as the log rolls on to its back and the rich dampness of humus flares our nostrils. Little creatures freeze in terror, like impala jacklighted on the farm track, frozen in a moment of their secret lives. Then they flee, each moving as fast as the legs particular to its kind allow. Wolf spiders scuttle headlong for several body lengths and, finding no shelter, stop and stand rigid, the milk-white, silken egg sac carried between the fangs of the she-wolf pulsating gently. Millipedes stop masticating their way through mould and coil their bodies into tight protective conchs. Earthworms writhe in the damp soil trying to bore their way into it. Now the colony has gone – life sucked out of the earth with the moisture. All that's beneath the log is the fossil of an old tunnel carefully spat together by termites. Cia stamps on it with her *takkie*. It crumbles to ashes.

As the months pass and the drought worsens, the reservoirs on the farm fall lower, and still we keep pumping water out of them. As the level sinks, more and more of the algae-slicked inner walls are exposed to the naked light of day for the first time. We hang over the rim and feast our eyes on what before was only half seen, half felt by toes. Now it blisters and peels to death, and still the suction valve keeps sucking. Mom stops all non-essential irrigation. It turns out that the garden is non-essential. The frail little petunias and pansies wilt and die limply, and a perpetual army of ants marauds across the russet lawn, leaving bare patches in its wake.

The *bushveld* looks desperate. Most of the trees of the woodland-savannah have shed their leaves, knowing that to survive winter they must surrender to a sort of half-death, and the ground is now bare of grass, so there is nothing to relieve the relentless brown and grey. Even the greedy mopane, who buds first and sheds last and secretes a mean, bitter tannin to stave off browsers, is now leafless. The trees in our Grimm

145

Brothers' books, which feature enchanted forests galore, look nothing like ours as it is. The enchanted forests are stuffed full of trees with names like oak and fir, thick of girth, their boughs groaning under lavish green leaves or furry white snow. Away from the riverine, where forests of mashatu, marula and fever trees look most like the enchanted forests of once-upon-a-time, the knob-thorn acacia and even the buffalo thorns that grow down in the valley take after something else. Cia reckons a tree's body tells the story of their life, same as a person's. Well, our trees' struggle for life sure has been a gruelling one. Gnarled and twisted, now stripped naked, they march into the distance like a grotesque army of cripples. It makes me squint to look upon this stark scene under the brilliant, hard blue sky.

Sometimes Cia and I march out with the army of cripples. Between their contorted skeletons low thorn scrub claws at our bare legs and we have to navigate the veld wreckage strewn everywhere: abandoned termite mounds, husks of dead trees, suspicious pits bored into the earth. We've started to find the carcasses of impala, nyala and even great kudu bulls lying there in the veld.

For animals like the buck that eat grass for a living, a drought is about the worst kind of dangerous there is. See, grass is a pretty feeble food – you can shovel down mouthfuls of it all day (and I'm talking the plump, juicy-stalked kind, never mind the golden dry thirsty kind), and it still hardly gives you enough horsepower to bother with the trek to the waterhole in the evening, fight the other buck, keep a look-out for lions and get on with the other business of living. So buck must eat almost all the time just to stay alive, which is one thing when the grass waves across the veld like a sea, but now, at the height of the drought, the buck and *mombies* have overgrazed the land to baldness, and as prisoners of our barbed-wire fences, unable to migrate, they are starving.

One day Cia and I even find a little bushbuck dead in the river. He can't have been dead long – he's still perfect. Once he's lain there awhile he'll start to melt into the earth, boiling with bluebottles and their maggots. We crouch to look at him, lying on a bed of river sand, the water streaming over his dappled hide, and I wonder how he could have endured the terrible hardship of the hinterland only to lie down and die on reaching the water – water that would have cooled his swollen tongue and which nurtures tender little seedlings and shoots of grass in its shallows as it shrinks inwards from lack of rain. I wonder what the bushbuck suffered and what he thought when he died and whether he loved his life. He stares back up at us, sinking softly into his riverbed coffin, and the water streams away his answers. There aren't even enough vultures, jackals and other scavengers to get rid of the carcasses. It's started to reek.

But if the farm and surrounding district look bad, the TTL look way worse. Mutambara is pretty barren even in good rains – little mud huts huddle in the dust that encrusts their scrawny, tick-ridden *mombies*, the skin sagging off their protruding hipbones, and the lonely acacia tree by the *kraal*. All the other trees have been hacked down, the veld is pitted with their stump scars, and when the wind blows, the dust cavorts across the land in mad, swirling dust devils. Oupa says it's 'cause the *munts* breed like flies and practise farming from the Dark Ages. Even in Mana Pools, the Lower Zambezi and other places that were saved from the *munts* for wildlife more than half a century ago, nothing grows on the great swathe of what was subsistence farmland behind the riverine, not even the hardiest of hardy pioneer weeds.

In good years, when the rain does fall, the flush of green grass that sprouts around the small *kraals* helps to hide the poverty of the people and the soil, and how the land is being eroded away to a spiny exoskeleton. It sure looks better than the shantytowns around the cities anyhow. What with the breeding like flies and everything, droves of young Africans, whom Oupa calls Dick Whittingtons, forsake the land to seek their fortune in the cities, but end up fortuneless in sprawling squatter camps outside them. In the slums, wattle and daub has given way to corrugated iron, scrap and tyres that hunker in a slew of rotting garbage. They have no sewers, no running water, no light at night, and Oupa says they are disease-ridden eyesores. Cia and I reckon that sore eyes has gotta be the least of your diseases in there, and if I was a Dick Whittington, I'd hightail it back to the TTL and grow me some nice *mielies* in the sun. But now, in the drought, maybe not. In the drought-stricken desert TTL, with its sunken, limp-eyed, parasite-infested animals and children, the *mielies* have withered away.

The Afs turn to *maranje*, the whites to praying. Never have the House of the Lord and the rainmakers enjoyed so many worshippers. But neither the spirits, nor the ancestors, nor God in His Heaven will give succour. Oupa says the

Earth has been forsaken by her gods, pagan and Christian alike. He grows maudlin in his gin-tinged musings as we look upon the thirsting world from the *stoep*. He, Oupa, has long prophesied this hour of reckoning. The Earth, who has been raped and plundered and who has had her lifeblood bled out of her, is now barren. That night the Earth becomes Satan's dominion – the realm of fire.

It comes upon us like a nightmare. I wake in the darkness to an acrid smell in my nostrils. It was entangled in my sleep, which had a faint glow at its edge, and even when I wake up, something of a dream still lingers. I can hear crashing and screaming from somewhere far away.

'Cia! Cia!' I whisper urgently in the darkness. 'Wake up!'

'Nyree?' Cia is groggy, groggy but panicky, as she rouses herself.

The faint glow on the horizon of my sleep has become an eerie irradiation. Flickering shadows are cast through the mullioned windows. With Cia beside me, I kneel on the bed beneath the Paisley swirls of the curtains to peer through the pane. The whole mountain is ablaze. A serpent of flame is snaking its way across the face of it, consuming the forest like a searing, cackling fiend. We stare out at it fearfully, mesmerized.

Suddenly Mom is in our room, dispelling the effect. Hurry. We must hurry. The fire will reach the farmhouse. We hurry. Downstairs, through the dark, stumbling after the pool of torchlight as it darts and flits before us and out into the ironic chill of the night. The Afs are running down the track from the *khaya*, which is ablaze. Adults carry babies, children

149

carry pots of food and smaller brothers. They are an unearthly river of black ghosts flowing before us. In the invisible swirling smoke, their cries seem disembodied, voices floating above the river.

'*Gijima! Gijima!*'

'*Shesha!*'

I stop running and look back up the mountain slope. The ground is boiling, flowing lava in the moonlight, dark trees seethe and bulge and burst into flame, spewing shards of embers into the sky. The lower terraces are moving – alive with baboon, bushbuck, squirrels, snakes, God's creatures spilling over the lip; leaping, slithering, crawling in desperation before the fire that hunts them. Even the smallest, lowliest beast that must crawl on its belly thinks its life is precious.

Mom is shouting in my face, shouting and pulling at my arm. I am running towards the trees that lead down to the river. As we reach the edge of the riverine, I remember. Where is Cia? Her hand is not in mine any more and I can't remember when I lost it. I look over my shoulder and see only the fire snake and its prey pouring over the lip of the terraced slope, and then I stumble and Mom is still pulling on my arm. Father, forgive me. I have lost Cia. It's like I've died and gone to Hell except that I haven't. I'm *alive* and in Hell.

We are the last to arrive. The whole farm is arrayed on the riverine edge, watching the conflagration. And then I see her. She's hanging over Jobe's shoulder like she's a freshly killed bushbuck. I tug on Jobe's sleeve until he pulls his eyes away from the fire and sees me waiting for him to put the dead bushbuck down. He lowers Cia and we stand together in the shallows of the river, her small hand in mine, and watch the last of the magic succumb to the firestorm. Then I turn away and find the moon reflected in the water. It's good, I think, to remember something of beauty before my eyes are burned out of my skull.

Hours later, the inferno dies down to a glowering smoulder. It dies before it reaches the farmhouse too. Cia is still next to me in the water, swaying. Mom is nearby. She whispers to us to go on back to sleep. As we retrace our steps through the front room, a moonbeam falls across the hearth. It draws my eyes to the old portrait of Great-grandfather. He stares down at me, patently alive, an accusation on his face. I feel deeply sorry for him – all that toiling, wasted for ever.

15

It's about the worst kind of bad there is. We're standing on the *stoep*, Cia and me, gazing sorrowfully at the naked mountain. Even though we watched with our own eyes the fire eat the forest alive, still the night had been mercifully draped over it. Now in the brittle morning light, the mountain lies bare, her secret groves and crevices exposed in a way that is indecent. Now I know why Great-grandfather de Beer wanted to smite them sinners for coming heedless of their nakedness into the sight of the Lord. It is a shameful thing. All of the underbrush has been eaten for tinder, leaving charred dead ground in its wake, and many of the smaller saplings have also fallen prey. Only the large canopy trees still stand – scorched black by tongues of fire and skeletal, the fate of their living marrows unknown till the next rains.

Cia and I have seen many, many veld fires over the years. Every winter the Afs set fire to the land: at night you can see the flames twisting like vines across the hills; in the morning, what was golden grassland is black, and by the end of winter, a sluggish phlegm hangs in the sky, murky as stagnant water, magnificently jewel-stained at sunset. Jobe says that to slash and burn brings new life from the earth, but at school it's been made plain that a fire-starter is worse even than a litter-bug (and you curl up your lip and spit out the word when you call someone a litter-bug) and any boy who is caught playing with matches will hear Mr McCleary's willow stick swish through the air before it lands on his match-playing backside. There are road signs everywhere sporting Bambi's face with a great big Bambi tear dripping down his cheek on account of people starting veld fires. Now after our own fire I know for sure that a fire isn't the bringer of new life. It is the bringer of death. No wonder the Devil has made Hell out of it – it is the first evil I have ever seen up close.

The Afs have had it bad too – the *khaya* is now just a spiny black ruin and there's been wailing and carrying on all day long because they have lost everything. One of the *picanins* – it was the little girl in the ripped purple dress – got burned in the fire. She has great suppurating weals on her face and chest where the skin blistered clean off. Oupa dabbed ointment on them while she screamed fit to burst a blood vessel.

The military police come by later that day and inform Mom that the suspected arsonists are terrorists. Cia and I hug the pillars on the *stoep* and stare shyly at the policemen in their blue uniforms. Now, for the first time, we have a reason to hate the Terrs. The Terrs don't dare attack the farmhouse out of fear of landmines on its perimeter, so they tried to take advantage of the dryness and burn it instead. Mom and the military police are of the view that it's fortunate the fire died

154

out before it reached the mountain's lowest slopes and the farmstead proper, but for Cia and me, the loss of our forest is maybe worse than losing anything else.

Cia's face droops as we trail dejectedly through the silken ashes seeking the earthly remains of the creatures too small, too frightened to escape, and solemnly marking their passing.

'Nyree?'

'*Ja?*'

'Do you think all the fairies got burned up?'

I lift the shell of a small tortoise and peer into it. I can smell the singed body of the tortoise curled up inside – his own house must have become the oven in which he roasted alive. I know she wants me to tell her they escaped. I look at her and shrug.

Dad comes home. His ambush falls kind of flat on its face. Then we tow after him through the ruins of the forest. Dad says lots of things about the *munts* that we aren't allowed to say.

'Jesus Christ!' and he whistles through his teeth. 'They'd destroy bloody Paradise itself if they were let in, the goddamned savages.'

Then he tells us to stop moping around like a pair of mongrels and it's not as though somebody died, and let's all get the hell out of here and go fishing, which is the only civilized thing to do under the circumstances.

Going fishing means going to Lake Kariba.

Lake Kariba, born of the Zambezi floodwaters, goes on for ever and ever, broken up only by islands that rise from the

155

depths like Atlantis with names that taste delicious – Tshinga, Spurwing, Fothergill. Sometimes great storms lash the waters into tidal waves. The Matusadona National Park that borders it teems with plains game, and in the endless cycle of life, which is the way of all things, the tree graveyard has become a roosting ground for great flocks of cormorants, herons, egrets, and a hunting ground for kingfishers, especially those who can't hover, and who use the grimacing, shit-streaked branches as watchtowers from which to spy prey. Over it all reigns the African fish eagle whose desolate cry, which resonates across the water at sunset, laments the slain Cocky Robin. Oupa taught me and Cia the song:

> *Zonke nyoni lapa moya,*
> *ena kala ena kala,*
> *ena swili, ena file,*
> *lo nyoni Cocky Robin.*

You howl the bit about him being dead and fallen, '*ena swiiili . . . ena fiiile*', but it's not nearly as sad as when the eagle cries for him.

It has to be said, though, that we see Kariba from far below where the fish eagle soars. We've seen a film about it at school. Every Friday afternoon we file into the hall, the class monitor gets to draw the velvet curtains across the high, dungeon-like windows with a long pole (I only once got to be class monitor, Cia never), and we sit in the darkness that crackles with static as the film reels are loaded. When at long last the bobbins start spinning, the screen flickers into a

156

countdown from five to an upside-down one, snuffing out the whispering crescendo, and *Operation Noah* bursts on to the screen.

In the first part of *Operation Noah* the great bowl-wall of the Kariba dam is built: colossal grey tombstones slowly close in the precipitous gorge – not without considerable loss of life, mind you. In the film we don't get to see the loss of life, but I make films of it in my head. Sometimes I dream about it. Men falling backwards through the air, like angels, falling for ever. I don't like to think about them entombed in the wall of steel and concrete. *Operation Noah* says the sacrifice of those men was worth it: they died in the building of a testament to the power and might of man over nature. But I still wonder what it would do to your soul, to be buried in the wall, imprisoned there for ever.

Then, in the next part of *Operation Noah*, the choked waters of the Zambezi river begin to rise, drowning the ancient riverine forest and savannah beyond. No one knew how fast the water would rise, flooding the Zambezi valley, giving the animals no chance to escape. They stand together on shrinking islands – even those that lived as enemies – shoulder to shoulder in death. They look strangely calm, a lot of them, the impala and wildebeest and whatnot, just lowing there, fear and bewilderment making them dull and bovine.

The elephants aren't so stupid as to stand there while the islands shrink into the water and they're all dead and drownded, like the sinners in the other Noah. They reckon on making a bid to save themselves. They plunge headlong into the swirling water and strike out for the mainland, swimming in long convoys, the big ones buoying the little ones with their trunks. I wonder how they can breathe and keep the babies afloat at the same time. Oupa says thousands sank to a watery grave, marked by the endless tree skeletons that now line the edge of the lake. Skeleton tree gravestones. We don't see them in the film either, the ones that sank. Instead we see the rescue operation.

Even though no one had predicted the flood that would come when the wall closed in, still, the men and machines – the very ones who, like God Almighty, had brought forth the flood – fought to save the lives of thousands of animals in peril. In *Operation Noah* they drive around in boats and helicopters saving animals galore. There's lots of flying low across the water and the sky, Afs running through the bush with long nets, bundling up animals who buck and struggle and look none too grateful for being saved.

At the end of *Operation Noah*, Noah's voice tells us – again – that this was a great triumph, not only for Rhodesia, which now has power to light up the highways and cities of the future, but for mankind itself.

Down on the ground where we are, me and Cia, Oupa and Moosejaw, it is grubby and shit-streaked like the dead trees, and it's easy to forget that there's another world above us. The first night we stay at the Caribbea Bay, which is a hotel like a cocktail drink with a slice of pineapple and a glacé cherry skewered on to a little pink paper umbrella. It's dazzlingly white, hums with air-conditioners, and sprawls through palm-treed gardens and cascading pools – nostril-singeing, eyeball-searingly clear from lashings of chlorine. It's a pity Oupa goes mad in such a fantastical place.

It's the whole concoction of stultifying heat in the Zambezi valley, gin and being so far from the *stoep*, to the edge of which his world shrank long ago, that has boiled Oupa's brain. What's curious, though, is that no one else seems to notice.

At first Oupa just made himself particularly disagreeable to everyone, especially the Caribbea Bay staff. It was like he was punishing them for having to be at the Caribbea Bay. He told the waiter at the pool bar, whose name is Forgiveness, that he was the worst waiter he had ever had the misfortune to meet and an execrable excuse for a human being to boot and that he, Oupa, would not rest until he'd seen to it personally that Forgiveness's arse was fired and escorted off the premises so that he could continue his pointless existence out of Oupa's sight – and all on account of Forgiveness not putting enough ice cubes in Oupa's gin. Cia and I saw Forgiveness scooping ice cubes galore into Oupa's gin, though, but they just melted as fast as ice-cream down your chin and on to the Peugeot seat in the car park at the Farmers' Co-op.

'He's just so mean!' Cia said.

Dad told Mom that Oupa's getting to be a cantankerous old bastard, but neither of them seems to notice that it's got far worse than cantankerous, unless cantankerous means stark raving mad. He spent all afternoon accusing Forgiveness of worse and worse things and complaining about everything on God's earth, which was no way

Forgiveness's fault. Then in the evening, he grimly summoned Cia and me to the toilet in our bungalow and pointed with a trembling, liver-spotted old hand to the baboon spider lurking inside it.

'*Sis*, man!' I hissed. Cia shuddered. But actually there was nothing uncommon about this: baboon spiders, snakes, scorps and all manner of *gogos* have always shown a partiality for the bog on the farm – it's nice and cool and dark in there, and if I was a baboon spider, I'd probably fancy it to lurk in. But Oupa didn't see the baboon spider's lurking there as being explained by baboon spiders' general partiality to lurking in toilets.

'See, lasses, there it is. I knew it. They're a-conspiring to get me!' His eyes bulged in their sockets.

Then he told Cia she could wipe that grin off her chops. The baboon spider had been deliberately planted there by the *munts* as part of an elaborate plot, which also involved the *tokoloshe*, to get him.

Mom and Dad not noticing Oupa's flirting with madness shouldn't really surprise me, since they hardly seem to notice Oupa at all. It is as if, to them, Oupa is there but somehow isn't – like something that hovers on the edge of their peripheral vision. Maybe that's how they can put up with him – by not really putting up with him at all. Cia thinks it's just what happens to old people. Adults say all sorts of pious and noble things about the wisdom of age and whatnot, but in truth, for old folks, it's like their story has ended before they have, and all that's left is the retelling – except they're not heard or even seen by the ones whose time it is, instead they're seen only by us, the ones whose time has not yet come – until the book finally closes on yesterday's story.

So Mom and Dad sauntered off hours ago, having doggedly ignored Oupa's increasingly outrageous complaints all day, to a dance at the Cutty Sark Hotel and now things have turned real bad.

We're in a court-martial. The accused – several unfortunate waiters, night porters, kitchen staff, me, Cia and Moosejaw, who've also fallen under suspicion – are lined up in a row on the lawn. Our crime, which is *alleged*, involves a convoluted series of related incidents that starts with the theft of Oupa's false teeth and ends in the sending of the country to the dogs. Oupa is lurching up and down the line of sullen-looking co-accused, brandishing a shotgun, lisping, 'So help me God, I'll rout out the bastard. Do you think I'm a-going to stand by and do naught while you *munts* filch me teeth, fleece the ruddy shirt off me back and then hand the country over to that Commie mad-dog Mugabe?'

He stands there, severing sagging strands of saliva with his tongue between his false-toothless gums, sweating with the effort of the interrogation.

'And stand to attention, boy,' he orders Cia, who has her head cocked to one side, her mouth hanging open in undisguised fascination. She snaps to attention and salutes smartly. Oupa grunts approval and moves on down the line.

But marshalling Cia is the last thing Oupa gets to do at his court-martial since at that very moment Mom descends on him like an avenging angel. She wrenches the gun from his grasp and orders him to bed at once. Oupa eyes her for a minute. While he is not normally inclined to obey anyone's orders, something in Mom's tone must have warned him that he'd maybe gone too far. Eventually he gives in, but not before turning back to his prisoners in the dock and dispensing one last apocalyptic warning: '*Ja*, well, you *munts* might "*Pamberi chongwe*" your way into that spineless, gutless sell-out of a government but, Holy Mother of God, you'd better not tread on my farm. If you think your ancestors are to be feared, you wait till you meet mine – they'll show you "*Pamberi chongwe*" all right, *comrades*!' With this he adopts a jaunty attitude and saunters off to bed incongruously singing, 'Gee it's *mush* to be back in the bush.'

Afterwards, Mom spends long hours apologizing profusely to the injured parties, and Dad is obliged to dole out considerable compensation so that the injured parties don't turn into plaintiffs. The plea bargain works and Oupa is not to be prosecuted by the hotel, but there is no plea bargain for Mom's wrath, and Oupa is hollered at something proper by her before being put on final probation. Since he can't be sent back to boarding-school, he will be sent to the old-age home if there's another episode like this one. Oupa doesn't seem very sorry to me, though. He looks like he'd like to brag about this episode.

In the morning we set off in Dad's motorboat for Tshinga Island. Tshinga is a remote place with a tented camp pitched in the shade of a grove of mashatu trees. The camp is deserted except for Thankful, the cookboy. We move in and soon it's like we've always lived there. At night we sit around the fire on the edge of the lake shore and watch the twinkling lights of the kapenta boats strung out across the horizon.

The boats have lanterns and great nets suspended like black sails from masts. These the fishermen lower into the waters to trawl for kapenta all night, helped by the lights to which the fish are drawn like underwater moths with shimmering scales. When the sun comes up, they return to shore where the fish are weighed. The fishermen line up in front of great scales to wait their turn. After their fish have been weighed, they click their tongues and shake their heads. Some shout at the scales boy. They call him a cheat. All of the fishermen tell long stories about the glorious size of the catches in days of yore, about the decks of the boats groaning under the weight of kapenta at dawn.

The fish are dried in the sun – the stench wafts out of the harbour and stinks up the whole place – then packed into bags, sold for a few cents and eaten with relish by the Afs. Dad says it's a source of protein that, for many on the edge, staves off kwashiorkor. We use it as bait.

Later, as Cia and I lie on our cots under the canvas, we listen to the ghoulish howling of the hyena. If we shine our torches into the darkness in the early evening, their eyes glow like those of demons as they stalk menacingly around at the edge of the camp. In the dead of night, though, after the fire has died to a few glowing embers and all is silent in the camp, the pack dares to trespass. We awaken to hear their sniffing, clawing and fiendish cackling outside our tent. Moosejaw whimpers. Our pulses race, but they never shred it, as they surely could, with one long claw flicked out of a paw. The rule is never, ever, leave the tent open – bush tales abound of hyenas entering open tents and ripping the faces off the sleepers within. At dawn they hear the prickle of the rising sun and fall silent, bloody and afraid. They slink back, creatures of the shrinking shadows, to await the end of day and its slow, stealthy stealing of the light.

In the mornings, we go fishing in one of the old fishing-boats moored by the camp. Mom makes some flimsy excuse, but Cia and I troop dutifully along only to be bawled out for the duration by Oupa for getting our lines tangled, losing our sinks, threading our worms on our hooks like sissies (since we're too squeamish to keep refolding and impaling them until their juices squirt out) and generally proving a bitter disappointment to him. On the third and last day, though – when we take Thankful along as chief worm threader – Cia catches the biggest bream of all, which redeems her marginally as a grandson. The fishing trip ends in disaster, though, as we get stuck in the maze of bulrushes during the excitement of Cia's great catch. Dad has to leap into the water to hack them from the propeller, then push us through a channel to the deeper water.

'Hey, you blokes better be on the lookout – I've only got one pair of goolies, you know.'

Thankful, who is punting the boat from the front, guffaws. 'Yes, Baas.'

'What's goolies, Dad?'

'Never mind. Just scout for flatdogs.'

'Okay, Dad.'

We go home, Oupa still in disgrace, and Cia and I, despite

164

vowing to stay sad for ever, considerably cheered up. We play rock, paper, scissors on the back seat of the car. Oupa makes up dynamite, which beats everything, and Cia has to give up the gap between the front seats. Moosejaw just lies there with his chin on his paws, lifting one eyebrow, then the other.

In the Eastern Highlands, as we leave the Vumba behind and head further south along the mountainous spine towards Chimanimani, I notice for the first time that the country grows wilder. Towns are sparse, replaced by towering milk-wood and *khaya* forests. Luxuriant ferns and wild orchids festoon the roadside.

When we get home, Ronin is lying in wait for us.

He has changed, though. He's got better at his act – and it's as though the actor can't tell himself apart any more. He fits his skin better; he doesn't seem like he's apologizing all the time. He looks right at you too, and he smiles a lot, although the smile isn't in his eyes. I know he's watching from behind them somewhere inside. Whatever torment he suffers at boarding-school – and not the chained-up-in-the-basement kind but the kind that comes from his faintly girlish chin and his silky voice and the delicate way he flicks his blond Barbie-doll hair – it has glazed his façade to a hard shininess.

Mom seems to like him even more. She told him, 'Welcome home,' and smiled and gave him a kiss, like it really is his home, and said he was quite the young man now. Ronin looked right pleased with himself. Oupa narrowed his eyes.

When we get upstairs I know we've had an intruder in our room: Grover has disappeared. He always sits propped up on Cia's bed, but now there is nothing except a slight impression on the pillow. Grover has suffered numerous misfortunes along the way, including the loss of one eye, then both ears in a brawl with Moosejaw, who is jealous of him, and is therefore in no position to fend for himself, according to Cia. We ransack the room but still he doesn't turn up, so Cia tells Mom tearfully that he's gone missing.

Mom says not to worry, she and Jobe will help us search for him – we'll be like a proper search party. Ronin says he'll join it. He'd walked into the kitchen and overheard the whole thing, but instead of ignoring it and us as usual, he smiles down at Cia and tells her that Mom's right, she needn't worry, that Grover loves her and isn't going to stray far from home.

'We'll find him, you'll see,' he promises her, sounding so confident that Cia looks hopeful.

We never do find Grover, though. We search for ages. Ronin searches longer than anyone – I almost feel bad for him that he doesn't find him. When Cia and I go to bed, tired and Cia heartsore, Ronin tells Cia how sorry he is, but that Grover's one night of delinquency should be forgiven and that he's sure he'll be home in the morning. He smiles at her and winks, and even Cia manages a crooked smile back, titillated by the image of Grover as a delinquent. Now as I lie here in the dark listening to the funeral of one of the *umkhulus* on the farm, the pulsating drums and ululating voices of

166

the women spiriting the old man to his ancestors, I ponder the change in Ronin. It feels real.

Three days later I find Grover dead. He's been slashed repeatedly and savagely across his belly and his stuffing oozes from the wounds. He was shoved under Ronin's bed. Cia and I kneel on the old wooden floorboards beside it and stare at each other, wordless and sick. I knew to come and look here. I'd known it since the day Grover had gone missing, but the voice inside me, telling me to come in here and look, wasn't loud enough.

I keep seeing him smile and wink at Cia, like they were sharing their own private joke. I am truly afraid of him.

I lift the bedspread once again – an old glass Consol pickling jar with something inside it stands next to where Grover had lain, and I can't help wanting to find out what's in it. I pull it out between the yellow bedspread fringe. A *mossie* lies dead in the bottom of the glass, some of Grover's stuffing next to her. She must have found her way in through the hole in the neck where the throwaway tin lid screws in, tempted maybe by some Grover sponge for her nest. She must never have found her way out. No one heard her panicked glass-Consol-jar pleas for help. She died on the stuffing nest. I look at her legs sticking out stiffly from her body. Was she lured? Why couldn't she find her way out? Was the lid screwed on before or after she died?

I unscrew the lid and gingerly take her out. I stroke her with my thumb. I feel the silkiness of the feathers she loved to preen, the delicate bones beneath them, but the thrumming of her heart in her breast has stopped.

With an oily feeling in my stomach, I pull out the last object way back in a corner under the bed. It's an old wooden cigar box of Oupa's. Inside we find a squirrel curled up in the corner. It's completely empty besides the dead curled squirrel. When I look inside the lid, there are marks etched in the wood – many frantic little scratches, in the lid of the coffin.

We back fearfully out of his room and, cloistered in our own, feeling its sanctity violated, I persuade Cia, her eyes huge with horror, not to reveal what we have found. I am far more afraid of this Ronin, with his gentleness and his secrets, than the bully-boy whose place he's taken and sense danger in exposing his secret.

And so we are bound in a deeper conspiracy of silence. I take to watching Ronin closely at mealtimes, when his Prince Charmingness is at its best. It is difficult to detect anything, although he eats as though he is starved; needy, greedy. But it is in the fleeting moments between masks that he reveals something of himself. In the instant when one mask falls away and before he's moulded the next, I sometimes see his face, and it is utterly blank. His eyes are vacant. There is simply nothing there. Somehow it is the absence of anything that is most chilling. The hairs on my arms rise. And then he changes.

He has become the changeling of the Grimms' fairytale nightmare.

16

'*H*ey, let's go down to the riverine.'

It's as if even Dell can feel how Modjadji is being smothered under a blanket, the air hot and stale. He's only just got here and he can't wait to get away. Cia and I can't wait either.

The riverine is the green mamba of dense, evergreen forest that slithers along the banks of the Nhzelele as it winds its way through our farm, its roots probing deeply into the secret river that flows beneath the bed.

I know the main reason why Dell wants to go down there today. It is because of the *n'anga*'s cave. Oupa told him that when he was a boy a mad old *n'anga* lived in one that lies behind the waterfall at the mouth of the stream, which, in wetter years, hurtles down a crack in the mountain.

At the point where the stream tries desperately to ford the river, it plunges over the edge of a sheer ridge, creating a waterfall higher than Cia and me standing one on top of the other before it pools sorrowfully in the river below. It is the best place to swim. The water is so cold it sucks the air out of you as you dive in.

Oupa says that the *n'anga* who lived in the cave wore a shiny Victorian suit, with monocle and top hat, there were deep fissures in his splayed heels, and he had a motheaten leopardskin draped about his shoulders. Cia and me reckon Oupa lies. Dell reckons that now the river's dry we'll finally get to prove it.

I go along with it since the plunge pool is at least an hour's walk away, especially if you tarry *en route* playing *toktokkie* – tapping the ground and waiting for the beetle to tap back in answer – or pivoting dung beetles on their dungballs to dupe them into bowling back in the direction they've just come and joining Moosejaw in barking at the baboons in the hills.

We arrive well over an hour after we set off, but are half sorry that we set off at all. The waterfall has vanished, of course, sucked up into the thirsty earth, and our wizard's cauldron of a plunge pool that elbows off the main river channel, with its cold, swirling unknowable depths, has shrunk to a miserable muddy wallow. Bubbles burp glumly on its thick skin. Some mysteries should stay mysterious.

On the far side, though, on the exposed ridge rockface, there is indeed the unmistakable mouth of a cave. Excitement prickles my fingertips.

'Go on,' says Dell. 'I dare you.'

Dell loves a dare. Last time he did one, though, he ended up bawling, trying to get away from MacGillavry's wreck.

MacGillavry has a gun and a one-eyed dog. The dog howls at the full moon and everyone knows that sometimes old man MacGillavry joins him in the howling. MacGillavry would snap your neck like a chicken's if he caught you so much as looking at his wreck. Jeremiah dared Dell to touch it – MacGillavry's wreck. Me and Cia were there.

'Is that all? Just touch it?' asked Dell, scornfully.

Jeremiah nodded.

'I could do more than that. I could do way more. I could pop the bonnet or something. I could get behind the wheel, if you want.'

Jeremiah looked at him coolly and said, 'No. Just touch it. That's all you have to do.'

'Easy,' said Dell.

'And don't worry. Nyree 'n' Cia 'n' me'll whistle when we clock the shotgun.'

Old man MacGillavry owns a junkyard on the outskirts of town. A lopsided sign on the chained gate promises 'Cash for Scrap' next to another that says, 'Keep Out! Trespassers will be Shot!' The yard is littered with scrap; weeds snare the rusting carcasses of cars and oil drums. There's a corrugated-iron workshop in the middle next to a sagging caravan with dirty lace curtains in which old man MacGillavry and One-eye live. I know what it will smell like in there: stale socks and porridge.

The wreck is perched on bricks in front of the workshop. It's a Corvette. Dell reckons a Corvette is a Hot Rod. But I don't know about that: it seems pretty cold and dead to me. It's always perching on those bricks – I've never seen it sporting a set of wheels – and by the look of it, maimed and scarred, it's never getting off them. But old man MacGillavry

171

loves it. His feet are always sticking out from under the dead Corvette while he tries to grease it back to life.

We came up from the back of the plot, along the old barbed-wire fence, and crossed the street in front of it. We stood in a huddle and watched the wreck watching us.

'Well, go on,' said Jeremiah.

'I'm going, man,' said Dell. 'I'm just getting ready, okay?'

He re-crossed the street and loitered nervously outside the gate. He kept making as if to dart through the tear at the bottom – he'd start forwards, duck, then stop and sort of scuff the dust as if that was all he had a mind to do.

'I knew he didn't have the guts,' Jeremiah said, a swagger in his voice.

Dell bent and ducked through the tear, then ran down the gravel driveway that led straight to the wreck. He reached it, slapped the buckled red bonnet and ran full tilt back down the drive. He crawled through the hole, snagging on the jagged wire, then bolted straight past us, not waiting to see if MacGillavry and his shotgun and his howling one-eyed dog were after him. We followed on his heels.

'Jesus!' It was Jeremiah. 'He's sicced One-eye on us! Run!'

He overtook Dell, who was trying to look backwards. Dell stumbled and fell headlong on the tarmac. He groaned, then hauled himself back up, but he was bawling now. Snot snorted in his nostrils as he ran.

We got all the way to the far end of the street before we stopped, doubled over, panting, and looked back. The old place was the same, hunched and surly, but as I peered closer,

I saw One-eye crouched behind the fence. He was utterly still, watching us, like he'd been there all along, except he hadn't. Then his ear twitched. Flick. And all was still.

Now the only thing Jeremiah remembers is Dell bawling.

'No! No, I didn't,' Dell stammers feebly.

'Oh, *yes*, you did. I *saw* you. We all did.' We were the witnesses. We nod gleefully.

This time, Dell's dared us, which is the easy bit.

'What if it's like quicksand and sucks us in and we can never get out?' asks Cia, melodramatic, not really believing it, though.

'It's not, man,' I say, with all-knowing disgust – the telling of horror stories is a privilege that Cia does not enjoy – as I wrench off my *takkies* and squelch barefoot into the mud. Dell's not about to miss out and a minute later he's squelching behind me. Cia squelches in last.

We've not gone more than a few paces, though, when a pitiful mewling sound halts us. We turn to see Moosejaw pawing frantically at the ground at the edge of the mud hole. He's wearing mud socks, so he'd clearly ventured into it and ventured right out.

'Come on, Moosejaw!' Cia calls, to encourage him.

Moosejaw looks pleadingly at her, then treads tentatively on the mud. Immediately he sinks a few inches, then his spindly legs splay as they slide out from under him. He yelps and scrambles backwards on to dry land. Dell bursts out laughing. Moosejaw can't bear to negotiate the treacle mud any more than he can bear to be left behind. It's a dreadful predicament.

'Come on, Moosejaw – you can do it!' I urge him, but Moosejaw refuses to budge.

'Oh, well,' I say, 'he'll have to wait here for us till we get back.'

Cia nods and we turn to continue across the basin, at which Moosejaw whines as if he's mortally wounded. We turn again to see him dash audaciously into the bog once more, slip and sprawl across it, legs flailing.

'*Ag!* Shame! Poor Moosejaw,' Cia cries. We wade over to where he lies in an ungainly heap and try to help him up.

'Okay, we'll carry him,' Dell decides. So we lift and lug him across between us, grunting with the effort. It can't be very comfortable for Moosejaw either, but he wags his tail unflaggingly the entire way.

When we reach the far side and deposit Moosejaw on a drying algae-clad rock, we see that the floor of the cave mouth is almost over our heads. We have to haul ourselves up over the lip, then lean down to haul Moosejaw up by the scruff. It's only once we've made it inside, sweating from the effort of hauling, that I remember to feel a superstitious fear.

We peer apprehensively into the gloom. Slowly our pupils dilate and we make out shapes and shadows. The cave isn't deep, maybe twelve or so feet, but it tunnels off at the back to who knows where and is no more than six foot wide, and while the roof is far above us, it probably isn't even a man's height. The floor and walls are rough hewn, cool to the touch and smell musty from years of damp. Then Moosejaw spies the mound of ashes at the back of the cave. We make our way over to it and kneel down just in front of them, crusty with their ancient secrets.

Cia gasps.

They adorn the small jutting rock ledges behind the ashes. Every conceivable outcrop is festooned with one. Human skulls, dozens of them, grinning in the darkness. There is a great pile of human bones stacked in the corner too – femurs and ribcages and vertebrae – and there are old assegai arrowheads and shards of pottery, leather and beads in the mêlée.

Cia recoils. She stumbles backwards in her haste to get away. I stay still but only because I have gone stiff with fright. Then it dawns on me: the Shangani graves. The Afs on the farm, especially the old *umkhulus*, often talk of the ancient Shangani graves in the hills, which, when the rains come, sometimes wash away, unearthing the skeletons, angering the ancestors. The earth is cursed because of this desecration. Maybe the old *n'anga* who once dwelled in this cave salvaged the skeletons that washed down into the riverine, maybe he tried to restore their sacredness by secreting them in this crypt. And now we have discovered the secret.

'Cia! Hey, Cia!' I whisper theatrically. 'Come back. I reckon it's the dead Shangani.'

Cia crawls over and we kneel together staring at the ranks of skulls, until Moosejaw feels the need to paw one off its ledge and grab it in his mouth.

'Hey, Moosejaw! Let that go!' I order him. He ignores me and tries to back away with the Shangani clenched between his jaws.

'Get him, Dell!' I shout.

We lunge and grab hold of him, then try to wrestle the skull from his vice-like grip. Eventually he relinquishes his prize and sulks off to the front of the cave.

'Yeuch!' says Dell, holding the now Moosejaw-gob-drenched skull. That violated the reverential air and we both giggle.

'Jeez, there's like *maningi* skulls here,' Cia says, with devil-may-care bravado to whitewash her earlier running away and stumbling and all.

Suddenly Moosejaw growls menacingly from his lookout at the entrance to the cave – an unmistakable intruder alert. Cia and I freeze, then turn fearfully to face whoever it is. Over the rim, a head appears – I can't see the face for the light behind it – followed by a friendly voice.

'Hey, guys, whatcha doing?'

Cia's face tautens. Ronin pulls himself up into the cave, crowding it with his bulk.

'Oh, come on, Moosejaw, you know it's only me,' he says to Moosejaw, as though that wasn't the very reason for Moosejaw's raised hackles and throat rumbling.

Why has he stalked us? I hear a warning voice inside my head.

'Hi, Ronin,' says Dell, sounding honoured.

'Uh, hi,' I stammer, trying to keep my outside-my-head voice sounding casual.

'Look what we found,' says Dell, importantly.

Ronin comes over, and we shuffle apart on our knees to make way for him. He whistles appreciatively when he sees

176

that we are in a burial chamber. I tell him about my Shangani theory.

'I think we should tell Jobe,' Cia offers, in the silence that ensues. 'The Afs will reckon that this lifts the curse.'

'Yes, yes, I suppose they will,' Ronin muses. Cia looks at him suspiciously, her eyes slitted as though she can make out his ulterior motive if her focus is narrow enough. Then he smiles at her, so warmly that I can see she's thrown off balance. 'Come on, let's get out of here,' he says. There seems no more point in hanging around so we turn and shuffle out in single file. Ronin helps us down and we squelch our way back across the mud, Ronin carrying Moosejaw easily. The dog's hackles are still raised, though, and he wears a scowl on his face. Suddenly he lets out a high-pitched squeal. Cia and I spin to see him grimacing in pain.

'Sorry,' mutters Ronin. 'I must've pinched his tail by accident.'

Cia looks perturbed but says nothing. Neither do I. We squelch on and reach the far bank without further incident. But before I can clamber out, I'm splattered with mud from behind. I turn to see Ronin lobbing another cowpat at Cia – he's grinning, and I can see that he's lobbing it deliberately without force. Cia turns, looks stunned then giggles a little uncertainly.

'Come on,' Dell yells. 'It's war!'

Unexpectedly, I find myself bending and scooping a handful of mud, which I sling at Ronin. Cia slings one ineffectually at him too, then aims one at Dell, which hits him squarely in the chest. Next instant, it has escalated to all-out battle. The air is thick with mud missiles, we are screaming and slithering in the bog. Moosejaw runs frantically up and down the bank, barking like a lunatic. Eventually we resemble the men we like to mould from mud and bake in the sun, only the whites of our eyes betraying our flesh-and-blood innards. We sludge our way down to the river channel and sink in fully clothed. Afterwards we trudge home, sopping wet, mud-stained and pleased with ourselves.

As we descend the last of the terraced slopes to come upon the back of the farmhouse, we see Oupa sitting on the *stoep* by the kitchen – he is on vervet patrol. Jobe leans in the doorway. I could swear that when he sees Oupa, Ronin stiffens reflexively. Oupa watches us approach. Just as we come within earshot, he observes, 'Hm, look at that, like a hog, fresh from scavenging down in hogs' hollow. It's unfortunate that mud splattering ain't where the resemblance to swine ends either.' It is clearly aimed at Ronin.

Ronin stands stock still and stares at Oupa for a long minute. Maybe it's the buoyed-up mood he's in, but then he does something he's never done before. 'Why me?'

Silence meets this retort.

Then Ronin, who is braver for the silence, asks again, 'Why am I swine?'

Cia and I stand just as still, bracing ourselves for what will come out of Oupa's mouth and we aren't even the swine who's been stupid enough to sass back.

'Same reason you'll never call the O'Callohan name your own,' Oupa says, real cold and carefully. 'Can't live up to it. There's something mean about you, boy – something mean

178

and shabby. You smell of dirty little secrets and lies, same as what you come from.'

Ronin kind of cringes and I glimpse the old Ronin once more. Then he turns and walks away.

I'm embarrassed in front of Dell, so is Cia. We just pretend the whole thing didn't happen. We scamper up the steps past Oupa and rush into the kitchen to tell Jobe of our finding. Jobe is mightily impressed, as he ought to be, by our revelation.

'*Eish*, little ones, this is a big *indaba*!'

The next day is Sunday and the day of rest, so Jobe and a party of *umkhulus* are elected to go down to the waterfall cave and see for themselves. Cia and I hang around the half-built *khaya* impatiently all afternoon awaiting their return, eager for our well-deserved glory. At sunset, Jobe and some of the others emerge from the woods carrying a trunk of some kind. We rush over.

'Well, Jobe, are they the dead Shangani?'

Jobe shakes his head noncommittally. 'Go inside now, little ones.'

We stand crestfallen as they parade solemnly past. It's a damn cheek, if you ask Cia and me. There we go a-risking our very lives crawling into the pitch black of that cave infested with who knows what kind of swamp creatures and *n'anga* ghosts skulking about in the shadows, find them the dead Shangani and all, and get told to bugger off for our thanks.

That night after dinner, Jobe mounts the steps of the *stoep* where we were all sitting – a highly unusual intrusion after dark. Cia and I sit up from our slump, interested in why he's intruding.

'Eh, *Mama*, eh, *Baba*.' He inclines his head towards Mom and Oupa.

Then, gravely he informs Cia and me that when he and the other *umkhulus* arrived at the cave, many, many of the skulls were smashed to pieces. Cia and I are shocked. We crane round immediately to see Ronin. He stands a short way off, watching us. Is that a smirk on his face? It is gone before I am sure, but he stares coolly at Jobe, then at us, and says sympathetically, 'God, how awful, can't imagine how this could've happened.' And we're thrown off balance again.

One thing I am sure of, though: he destroyed those skulls and, what's more, I am sure that he knows we know. This isn't like Grover's death, which he desired to keep secret. This time he's committed an Act of Profanity of which he knows we must suspect him. The silence between us is some sort of test, a game he's won. It's given him power. And Mom is blind to all of it.

17

'Invective' is a word that means poison from your lips. Oupa spits invective at Ronin like a serpent and we're going to pay. I know it in my gut and it's my gut that's just waiting for pay day to come.

Me and Cia and Oupa are on the *stoep* drinking Mazoe orange juice, Oupa sulkily: he isn't allowed his first gin until after sunset now and Mom decides when the sun has set. He has been sulking fit to bust his britches ever since she imposed the damn sunset rule, which is a torment that not even Satan and his Foul Minions would inflict upon an old man who was, anyway, just minding his own business. We sure wish she hadn't. He tells us that he only drank to make the rest of us seem interesting and we grimly slurp our Mazoes.

Moosejaw chooses the slurping moment to declare his love and loyalty to Oupa. He prances up on his hind legs and pummels Oupa with his paws, panting and wagging his tail so hard it might wag right off. Oupa shoves him away and brusquely tells him that he is a disgrace to his canine species, a disgusting little rotter that not even the *munts* had wanted – and they'll eat anything.

He scowls.

'There is grovelling here, lasses. There, grovelling for love. Pathetic. Do we have any more shameless little grovellers here? Speak now.'

There is no speaking.

'Do you think your great-grandfather went about grovelling on his belly for anything 't all in his whole life? Speak now if you think your great-grandfather went about grovelling.'

There is no speaking.

'Grovelling is a shameful thing and O'Callohans are not known for shamefulness. The *munt*, on the other hand, now there's a miserable groveller for you. Starts grovelling when his mam's still wiping the snot from his nose and he's still grovelling when Beelzebub's stoking up the inferno for him on Judgement Day. Now, what is it the O'Callohans are not known for?'

'Grovelling on their bellies and general shamefulness, Oupa.'

'Now if I hear of any more grovelling around these parts the stick will come out. What will come out, lasses?'

'The stick, Oupa.'

'The stick will sting, lasses. The stick will sing through the air, it will land on the backside of the groveller caught grovelling on his or her belly. Where will it land, lasses?'

'On the groveller, Oupa.'

'Busted doing what?'

'Grovelling on their belly, Oupa.'

He looks down at Moosejaw. 'Now, bugger off! Don't you know you can't beg for love? You're just a freeloading little bloodsucker, of no use to man or beast, and here only by the grace of that bleeding-heart daughter-in-law of mine. If it were up to me, you snivelling little wretch, your kennel would be six feet under!'

Moosejaw carries on pummelling Oupa joyously, blind to the sorry business of his being a disgusting little rotter, a groveller and a freeloading bloodsucker who's been spurned by the object of his affection. Oupa lets him.

The next day Cia and I are clambering over the first terrace wall; Jobe has told us that the season has turned, and even though we can't yet feel a change in the air, we know from past years that Jobe has a weather vane inside him, and that if he has forecast spring, then spring is springing even as he says the words. We're going to inspect the barren terraces for evidence.

We don't find spring, but squatting in the dirt we spy on a slave raid. The ground around us boils with ants: red ants locked in mandible-to-mandible combat with black ants. The slavers are the red ants. The black ants lie dead and dying around their nest; the maimed fight bravely on. The red ants will destroy the black ants' army and capture the cocoon-clad pupae, whose instinct, when they hatch, will tell them to accept their nest mates – so they will enter into voluntary slavery of their captors. I don't want to watch any more. I feel sorry for the black ants.

As we round a large boulder, still veiny with the exposed roots of a wild fig tree, we get hissed at.

'Hey! Hey, you two brats!' Ronin whispers hoarsely.

We turn to see him crouching on his haunches in a small gully scoured out under the far side of the boulder. He seems to be concealing something between his legs, and as we lean over, we see that it is Moosejaw. Ronin has tied a rope around his neck. Moosejaw seems strangely subdued; he stands still, his head hanging – submissive. When he spies us, he wags his tail nervously by way of greeting, but that is all. Maybe he senses danger and figures that if he does absolutely nothing to goad Ronin he can somehow ward it off.

Ronin rises on his haunches. He eyes us as we take in the scene, which has an unmistakably staged feel about it. Then he says, real slow and deliberate-like, 'Well, now, you heard your grandfather, didn't you? I mean, you were there, weren't you? Sitting there like two fawning little puppy dogs licking his feet. So, what was it he said?' He cocks his head. 'Hmm. Yes, yes, that's right, now I recall: "Nobody wants a parasite, do they? Leeching off everyone's guilt, do they?"' His voice, normally so honey smooth, now drips with Oupa's invective, spitting it back up.

'Shameful bastard mongrels should have kennels ... What did he say? What did he say? Six feet under, I believe it was.'

He breathes heavily after delivering his performance. Cia and I imitate Moosejaw and stand mute as he distorts Oupa's words. I didn't really understand them when Oupa said them and I didn't know that Ronin was there spying on us when he did, but I do understand that they mean something bad.

'So, you see, I've decided to do ol' Oups a favour. I haven't got enough chores round here anyway, so I'm making it my job to help him rid the place of vermin,' he finishes. Then he steps on to the terrace and yanks at Moosejaw's noose. Moosejaw bounds up after him, eager to please.

'Well, come on, then,' he invites us, in a new syrupy voice.

Ronin leads the way up the mountain slope. Moosejaw, Cia and I form a reluctant procession behind him. I have a sinking feeling in my stomach, like a powerful undertow. I am fearful, and the fear seems to have dulled my brain. I trail dully after Ronin, unable to think or do anything else. Cia seems equally stupefied. She trails in my wake, dread on her little face. Moosejaw, his tail between his legs, doesn't even turn around to look back at us.

The late-winter afternoon sun, insipid though it is, still soaks into the black earth until it radiates heat – sweat trickles down between my shoulder-blades as we labour up the steep slopes. It drips into my eyes and turns Ronin into a stinging, shimmering mirage. I taste the saltiness of evil on my tongue. At last we approach the charred skeletons of a clump of Msasa trees and Ronin slows. As we enter the dead grove I see just ahead of us a freshly dug hole in the earth. It is about two foot square but several inches deeper. Then I see the revolver lying at the base of a tree. I have a clear premonition of what will happen next.

Up until now the procession has been solemn, like we're in church, but Ronin is done with church. He seizes

Moosejaw by his scruff and shoves him brusquely into the hole. Moosejaw doesn't even protest; he sits on his haunches, the tips of his ears just sticking over the edge of the hole as he stares at Cia and me. I wonder about that. Why does Moosejaw who once fought fit for a mad dog to save himself just surrender now? Why doesn't he rush at him and bowl him down like a skittle and eat his face off while he's flailing about in the dirt? Why don't we? The look in his eyes betrays no fear, though. There is no desperation in them either. He stares straight at us. Does he seek comfort? Is it for courage? He does not even look at Ronin as he trains the gun on him. Cia and I hold his gaze. When Ronin squeezes the trigger, Moosejaw never even makes a sound. The bullet rips into his body. He jerks once and lies still.

At that moment I hear a strangled cry from Cia. She wrenches away from me, and runs backwards down the mountain slope. I run after her and catch her a short way off as she stumbles. She is retching and then vomiting into the dirt. The stones are slicked in yellow bile. I kneel by her trying to hold her, the tears blurring my eyes and clogging my throat, my breath rasping in my ears.

Ronin, who froze in the act of pulling the trigger, suddenly comes out of his stupor. He lopes towards us, and as he closes in, I see his face is terrible. I don't care any more. He grabs my hair, wrenches my head back, and I feel the roots tearing. Then he snarls savagely at me, 'Don't you ever, ever breathe a word of this to anyone, do you hear me?'

I just stare back at him, too stunned to do anything else.

'If you do, I'll . . . I'll . . . You saw! You saw what happened, to . . .' he says, in a strangled voice, almost as though he is afraid of himself. Then he seems to regain control. He gives my hair one last wrench, turns and flees down the mountain.

Cia and I stay where we are for a long time. Cia rocks backwards and forwards, the tears streaming silently down her face. I hold her in my arms, I try to comfort her, but I am sobbing; my whole body is racked with sobs.

Eventually, as the shadows are lengthening, we get up from the dirt and climb back up to Moosejaw's open grave. We just know to do it. We stare down at his small broken body, both silent, and then, with a great shuddering sigh, Cia says we should bury him properly. We cover him with our bare hands; the earth tears raw flesh from my soft palms, grit gets bedded in deep under my fingernails and slowly Moosejaw's fur coat becomes a coat of soil. Like he's just garbage. The last thing I notice is that his lips are curled up a little; a mongrel Elvis Presley. When the job is done, we stand together by his graveside not knowing what to do. Then we chant what we can remember of the 'Ah Father'.

After the 'Amen' we slowly descend the mountain. Cia's dirty, tear-streaked face is lit by the last rays of the sun.

18

Mom thinks our melancholy is because Moosejaw has run away from home. On the first night that he didn't come home for dinner, I could see she was worried. Moosejaw'd never missed even the whiff of food before. Nevertheless, she tried to tell herself, by telling us, that he'd just roamed too far, had got himself lost, and would no doubt find his way home sooner or later – bedraggled and hungry, but unharmed. Two nights later when there was still no sign of Moosejaw, who'd be worse than grubby and hungry by now, she began to really worry for him. The next day, she saddled up two of the horses and went out scouting for him with Jobe. They returned home late that same day, the lines around Mom's eyes etched deeper with dirt and tiredness. She summoned all the farm labourers the next morning, and offered a reward to anyone who knew anything about his whereabouts. Still no one has come forward.

I know why the lines around her eyes are so deep. She's spooked, and it's not just 'cause Moosejaw's gone. It's why he's gone that's got her neck hairs raised. I sat on the stairs winding my arms through the banister and listened to her quarrelling about it with Oupa the night after the scouting. When the Terrs are going to attack a farm they send a sign. The sign is the murder of the farm dog. Then they stick the dead dog on a stake at the border of the farm. Oupa reckons the Terrs got Moosejaw. Mom kept saying, no, that he wouldn't have just vanished like he has, that the Terrs wouldn't have just killed him: they'd have made sure we saw his mutilated corpse – so, no dead body, no attack. But I can tell she's scared anyway. Like Oupa kept saying, 'One way or t'other, that dog's vanishing's ill-omened.' He's right.

On the fifth night, Jobe, battered old trilby in hand, his face sober, mounts the steps of the *stoep* where we are all sitting.

'*Eh. Eh, Mama*,' he addresses Mom slowly. 'I am wanting tell you . . . is no good. The *inja*, he is gone. Something bad, very bad is happening to that *inja*.'

He says nothing after that for a time. Then he shakes his head ponderously and says something strange. 'I am thinking it was the jackal. It was the jackal, he killed him.'

The *n'anga* of Great Zimbabwe floats into my thoughts.

Then he swivels his head slowly and deliberately and stares straight at Ronin, who is hovering on the edge of the conversation as he always does whenever Moosejaw's name is mentioned.

There is a long silence. Jobe stares intently at Ronin. Ronin averts his gaze.

Then Mom sighs, raises her own lowered gaze, and says, 'Yes. Thank you, Jobe. I was beginning to fear as much.'

Cia and I remain stiff and silent throughout. Every time Moosejaw's name is spoken, Cia's face goes into rigor mortis and she stares rigidly ahead until his name passes out of the conversation. After Jobe's veiled pronouncement about Moosejaw's fate, though, something fractures inside her.

In the morning, she and I are sitting at the edge of the garden where the blackened terraces begin. Only dead things belong up here now. Cia is concentrating on the ant-lion craters, trying to rescue a trapped ant with a twig. She is busy coaxing it on to the twig life-raft when Jobe's shadow falls across us. As we look up he hawks self-consciously and we know that he wants to talk to us. He squats down on his haunches and, after hawking again and spitting on the ground, he squints at us in silence. Cia and I squint back at him. Then he says it: 'The *inja* Moosejaw is with the *mudzimu*.'

I want to believe it, but I never heard of a dog joining the host of ancestral spirits, so I'm sceptical and my scepticalness douses my desire to believe. Jobe inclines his head gravely in the face of my doubt and says more. Moosejaw is of the *mangozi* – the spirits of ancient warriors – who merely took the form of the *inja*.

Cia looks deeply impressed. After weighing this up for a moment, even my doubts are quashed: it's common among the dead to appear in animal form – they're as apt to do so as they are to commune with the living through dreams or omens or *n'angas*, and that Moosejaw is a *mangozi* explains his nobleness of spirit.

191

Now that Moosejaw has returned to the land of the dead, he will be our spiritual guardian. He will protect us from evil – it was never the other way round. Also, we can pray to him whenever we want.

'Whenever we want to?' Cia asks, hopeful tears flowing freely down her face.

'The only time you do wrong to the *mudzimu* is to forget them,' intones Jobe.

His words are a salve to Cia – to me, too. That Moosejaw only came to this earthly realm as a visitor from the spiritual one lends his death a sense of being predestined. It was his destiny – his body was borrowed, like his time on earth. And his guardianship is a thread that binds us across the realms.

Yet for Cia it is not enough. I know she thought much about what Jobe had said in the days that followed, and although his words – that death is not death – brought her peace, she still believes that Moosejaw was wronged.

It is night time and we are kneeling on my bed, draped once more in the secret shadowy space beneath the bottle green Paisley swirls of the curtains, our faces pressed against the cold pane. She turns to me and whispers, 'Nyree, what if he turns into the *ngozi*?'

Sometimes, after someone is murdered, their spirit is somehow corrupted by what happened to them in the flesh. The ghost becomes vengeful, evil. The Afs fear the haunting of the *ngozi*. Cia's rummaged through our treasure trove of African lore and dragged out the *ngozi*, and now I shiver at the apparition of Moosejaw, eyes glowing like demonic coals, hackles raised, fangs bared and snarling, blind to Cia and me whom he had once loved, his soul as black as night.

I tell Cia, with as much contempt as I can muster, not to be so stupid, man, but she can smell the fear on my breath.

'How do you know, *hey*?'

''Cause Jobe didn't say so,' is clearly grossly inadequate.

We lapse into silence, both already haunted by the spectre of our beloved murdered Moosejaw caught in the throes of the endless dark night of the soul. But Cia is not the only initiate in the cult of the dead. I hit upon our salvation.

'Cia. Hey, Cia, we need to do a *murombo*.'

A *murombo* is a purifying ritual for a contaminated place. Once the Afs performed the *murombo* ceremony by the tree in which Jonsai, who used to work on the fence line, hanged himself, since his restless soul left the place at night and roamed abroad, preventing people from walking to and fro their *kraals* of an evening. Passers-by saw flickering lights in the woods and heard the faint sound of screams – the sound seemed to be in front of them, but when they'd gone a little way, it seemed to come from behind. Anyway, since spirits stay in and about the grave for a time, it makes sense to consecrate the ground where Moosejaw died.

Cia almost seems to expect this.

'*Ja! Ja*, let's do a *murombo*,' followed immediately by, 'When are we gonna do it, Nyree?'

It is as though Cia is now the leader – I am merely doing her bidding.

'Um, on the next full moon.'

I have no idea when full moon is supposed to be. Cia goes

along with it, though: full moons always augur well for magical rites. Then she adds something strange and ominous. 'Only when he's said he's sorry, sorry for everything,' she hisses fiercely. 'Only then can Moosejaw forgive him.'

I shiver with understanding. This is not just to be an exorcism. Cia thinks that the evil can be purged only if there is atonement for the sin.

19

'When's the next full moon, Oupa?'

'How the ruddy hell should I know? Do you think I've got time to sit around staring at the moon every ruddy night?'

There are folks – mostly wastrels and also weirdos and Satan-worshippers and the like – who have time to sit around moon-gazing, but Oupa'll have us know that he does not number among them.

Cia looks balefully at him, then says to me, in a loud whisper, 'Okay, we'll ask Jobe. *He*'ll know.'

Cia and I never speak of Ronin. Apart from Cia's veiled words about his part in the *murombo*, she never mentions him, and I carefully avoid doing so too. If I catch his eye in the strip of light from his closing door, I pretend not to. I hate him. He fills me with fear, but it is more than that, more than just fear. The secrecy that shrouds what is between us binds us. We are intimate in a sordid way. It makes me feel soiled. I hope Cia's feelings for him are cleaner than that – just pure, clean hatred.

We speak of Moosejaw often, though – 'Hey, Digby, *voet-sek*! Moosejaw'd tear you apart limb from limb if he caught you scoffing from his bowl.'

Jobe tells us that the full moon is almost a whole month away. It feels like I'm being let off a sentence. I know that Cia is determined: to her the *murombo* is a duty that she can't shun, the way Oupa can't shun the duty of his father and his father's legacy, and I know that I will perform the *murombo*, for it is sacred, but four weeks is a long time and I'm free for all of it.

It's Saturday, Dad is back home from call-up, and we're going for a picnic at Mermaid's Pool with the families from our district. I suspect that we're going as a way of forgetting about Moosejaw. A forgetting ploy of Mom's. Ronin makes an excuse not to go, and we're all relieved – even Mom, I think. Maybe she's tired of all that pleasantness. She just says, 'Right, then, suit yourself.' And for the first time in ages, the mood is lighter, the shadows that have hung over us thin – they wisp like fine mist at the edge of my brain – and hanging on to the back of Dad's old Landie, in the early summer sun, singing 'We're Back In The Sticks' off-key into the wind, life is good. After the bleakness of winter, it is like swimming back into the warm treacle of summer, the cicada-ringing, miraged bush and all things worn familiar and comfortable.

The main attraction at Mermaid's Pool is neither a pool nor, to my disappointment, a mermaid. In fact, it is a river rockslide that plummets into a deep plunge pool at the bottom. The rockslide is hundreds and hundreds of metres long and real steep too. It is navigable by fat tractor-tyre inner tubes or bare bottoms – but bare-bottom is strictly for boys whose bravado outstrips their stock of common sense. There are loads of them here today.

While the adults lounge about under the trees, the throng of boys, me and Cia mill about at the edge of the pool, the boys boasting fit to burst.

'Last time I went down head first!'

'*Ja*, so, so big deal. I went down *backwards*!'

It is Dell who reckons he went down backwards.

'No, you *didn't*,' retorts Jeremiah, disgustedly. 'You were a big scaredy-cat. You wouldn't even stick your hands over your head sitting down. You only ended up backwards 'cause you flipped.'

Swapping brags for insults has the effect of egging on the bragging, and there's no end to the bravery and daring that went on last time – no one didn't go down headwards or backwards or some manner that needed shovel-loads of it. At the same time, the accusations of cowardice get meaner. Cia and I are dismissed as unworthy opponents – no bravery, no daring, don't remember who was a cowardy-custard. Cia just watches with her cheek-squashing grin plastered all over her face. We're not even a good audience for showing off to. I don't care. After a while it turns ugly: every past incident involving gutlessness of some sort is dredged up. No one forgets – ever.

Dell tells everyone that Jeremiah lost a wrestling match with Barry Swanepoel on purpose because he was scared of his big brother who's a prefect. 'What a sissy!' he says disgustedly.

'Well,' Jeremiah says heavily, 'at least I was never a fairy.'

He says 'fairy' in a whiny voice. You can tell he's got Dell from the way red blotches blossom all over Dell's neck. He was a fairy in the school play. He was the only boy fairy, named Puck. Miss Lovemore made him do it. There were girl fairies galore. I was one of the girl fairies. I got to wear a tutu with tinsel stuck round the edge and matching wings that Mom made out of a mozzie net. I looked real glittery. Even Jobe said so. He sucked in his breath and said, '*Eish!*'

But Dell was the only boy fairy. I didn't even know there were any until Puck came along. When Miss Lovemore told Dell he was chosen, he just stared at her. Then he licked his lips and spoke in a hoarse voice. '*Me?*' he said. '*Me? Me* be a fairy?'

'We'd be ever so grateful to you, Dell,' said Miss Lovemore, in a sugary tone.

On the night of the play there was a surging crowd of small boys at the front of the stage. Anyone who'd ever known Dell had come to guffaw at him in his green satin stockings and neck ruffle. Jeremiah and the Dogs of War had sworn to be there. You couldn't even hear Dell say his lines there was so much guffawing going on. Dell blushed for pure shame.

Dell ended up in Mr McCleary's office over it. The next day he put up his fists in the playground and said he'd fight anyone to the death who pranced on tippitoes and flapped their wings at him again. He ended up in a brawl with

Jeremiah and Sinbad. He rolled around in the dirt with them while a ring of boys chanted, 'Fight! Fight! Fight!' above them.

At the end of big break, when the whole school lines up in rows at the bottom of the steps, his name got called out with the usual boys who had to report to Mr McCleary's office. Most of them are in Standard Five, except Damian Gilchrist. Even though Dell acts tough, his name isn't normally among them.

I pretended I'd lost my hat and had to go to Lost Property so I could see him. He was lined up with the mooners and the spitters and the other fighters outside Mr McCleary's big oak-panelled door, looking scared witless. I felt real bad for him. Girls don't get the cane, only boys. Girls just get the ruler slapped across the palm of the hand, which isn't so bad.

After he got back to class, he sat gingerly on his chair but he looked kind of pleased with himself at the same time. He knew that getting the cane was one way of wiping out the fairy costume.

Now he narrows his eyes and says to Jeremiah, in a dangerous tone, 'If you say that one more time, I'm going to shove you over the edge of the slide so as you end up going down face first without even meaning to!'

'Oh, *ja*? Well, I dare you to go down face first yourself!'

Soon everyone's daring everyone else to go down face first and whatnot. Only Damian Gilchrist doesn't dare anyone. He doesn't need to.

The other boys are laughing, pushing each other, trying to trip each other. After jostling enough to pump themselves up, the boys, with me and Cia in tow, make their way to the top of the rockslide. Everybody's quiet now. I am terrified. From up here the rockface has tilted. It is steeper than it was below and stretches away into the far distance before it sinks into the abyss of the plunge pool. The current is fierce.

'Jeez, man, it's more like Victoria Falls,' breathes Dell.

There is nothing but breathing for a few minutes. Then Damian Gilchrist howls like a werewolf and throws himself off the edge. Soon the rest of the pack of boys is braying and throwing themselves down after him. Dad joins us, which helps. He spins us round in our inner tubes in the eddying rockpools above the slide while we wait for the queue to dwindle to the stragglers whose fear has whitewashed their desire to show off. It is Cia's and my turn.

Of course I have to go first. I wish I didn't. Dad manoeuvres my tyre tube out into the current with me wedged awkwardly into its squeaky, rubbery cavity, quaky with fear. 'Now, you grip on to that tyre, my girl, you hear me? Grip on!'

He shoves me off the lip of the slide. I career down the water chute, my tyre skittering out of control, spray spewing in every direction and me gasping with fear. Not an instant later, my tube hits the plunge pool and I surf into it on a wave, weak and high. It's brilliant.

I float around the pool with the boys, who are celebrating victory over the forces of nature and their own fear by thrashing noisily about in the water. I look up, anxious: it's Cia's turn next. As I squint up into the sun and the glare off the water, she appears a mere speck in the distance as Dad lines her up, so I must be imagining the fear on her little face. I have no more time to imagine it, though, as Dad has rushed her out over the edge and I see her hurtle down the rockface, her tube spinning wildly as she gathers momentum. I hold my breath. Everyone is treading water, watching silently too.

Suddenly Cia's tube strikes a ridge and, in slow motion, I see it flip up at right angles and over. For a heartbeat Cia is flailing through the air and then she hits the rock hard and is jettisoned forward, back into the current and downwards head first. As she plunges into the pool at the bottom of the shaft, I hear my first ragged gasp.

My eyes are riveted on the spot where she went down and I become dimly aware of Mom's hoarse screaming as she runs towards the riverbank. It is for ever since she struck the water and disappeared beneath it, but as I stare at the spot, two bedraggled blonde pigtails break the surface and Cia's head emerges, her green eyes saucer-like. She looks slowly around and then she does something totally unexpected. She giggles.

Once she starts giggling, she can't stop. It gurgles up inside her and spills out over all of us. It is infectious, too, and next thing I am laughing, but hysterically, with her. I dive out of my tube, swim over to her and, putting my arm around her, half drag her, still giggling and now swallowing water and choking, to the riverbank. Mom has waded right in. She lifts Cia and carries her out. Dad comes running up looking frantic and then hugely relieved when he sees Cia.

Damian Gilchrist swims over to where we are on the bank. 'You all right?' he asks.

Cia nods.

'Cool.'

Cia is a legend now. Among the boys. It was death-defying, her feat, and she laughed in death's face, and Damian Gilchrist went out of his way to talk to her and he said, 'Cool.' And as indifferent as Cia was to the boys' scorn before, she seems to revel now in her new-found reputation. Me, though, I am almost tearful that she is okay. I swallow the tears.

After that, the picnic carries on. The dads *braai* the meat over an open fire. We find a chameleon in the foliage by the river and proceed to plant him on every surface from rocks to leaves to my technicolour towel to provoke him to change colour. He claws his way up Cia's arm, his little eyes swivelling independently of one another, and then on to her head. She struts around, oblivious of the discomfort of claws embedded in her scalp. In the no-guts-no-glory stakes, she has guts and glory galore.

We are riding home into the last rays of the setting sun, burned and tired and content. The day has a sort of glow about the edges. Perfect. I feel it searing on to my brain the way something does when you know you'll always remember it.

20

When we arrive home in the evening, the light cast over the dying day is strange: everything is bathed in amber – the whitewash of the farmhouse is tinged with it, blurring the edges. Then the wind picks up. It gusts hot and angry down the mountain and batters the farmstead. As darkness falls, a great black bank of fearsome cumulo-nimbus rolls off the crags, lacerated by streaks of lightning. Thunder erupts through the lacerations, threatening to burst my eardrums. Finally, in the darkness, the storm breaks; the rain falls in heavy sweeping sheets until the earth, baked to a tough, leathery hide by the sun, turns soft and pulpy and the lawn under the security spotlights becomes soggy and water is pouring down the mountain in rivulets and the old dried-up watercourse has become a torrent roaring down the gully.

In the morning, the grey sky curdles and everything looks washed, washed of its red, scratchy dust crust, and the cracked scab that was the earth is rich and nurturing again.

Soon the soil will give way to sweet, wet plants. Cia and I go exploring every day. The forest is coming back to life. Plants we thought had surrendered to death send succulent rootlets probing through the spongy soil and unfurl plush new plumage. The canopy closes in again, the forest floor is a green tangle, plants fight viciously for light, for air, hungry for life.

The four weeks are up. Cia – who is the forager for knowledge, 'Do animals cry without tears?', the bearer of cruel truths, 'You only got to look at the TTL to know that God don't like Afs and that's what you get for being the tribes of Ham, but I reckon God doesn't like us any better, because I tested him and he is deaf where my prayers is concerned and I don't reckon Father Christmas is listening either' – is also the avenger of injustice, and she has not forgotten.

I have been pretending to forget – I sank myself deeply into the forest's resuscitation so I wouldn't have to think about it. I have a bad feeling about the *murombo* and I wish we don't ever have to do it. In the daytime I don't believe that Moosejaw will turn evil and I don't think we need to consecrate his grave so that he may rest in peace. But there is no way I can persuade Cia of that now – and I am afraid to anyway. She is so righteous: it feels cowardly even to suggest it, cowardly like surrender.

So now, on the night before the full moon, when it is already hanging like a distended bladder in the night sky, Cia and I are making final preparations. From Jobe, for the ceremony, I got some *msese*, which is beer brewed specially from *mielies*. It's fermenting in a scoured butternut gourd under my bed and Cia has stolen a box of matches from the pantry for what we don't know, and now I have to invite the last guest.

Since the day Moosejaw died, we have hardly said a word to Ronin. I try not to look at him. I know that he watches us, though, watches for our silence. Even as he sits at the dinner table, pretending to laugh and being all polite in the passing of salt and suchlike, I feel his eyes surreptitiously on us – like a rat sniffing us out, sniffing, sniffing. Now I have to approach him. It takes courage. My feelings for him are complicated, confusing, but my overpowering sense is fear. Still, after dinner I lie in wait for him behind the potted palm in the hall. When he comes down the stairs and heads out, as he does every night, I step out and accost him.

'We're going back tomorrow night. Tomorrow, just after the sun goes down, we're going back to the place where he died, where you – you killed him,' I hiss. I can't help the words that spurt out of my mouth.

Ronin goes rigid.

'And you have to be there, okay? So – so you'd better be there, at his grave, just after sunset. We'll be waiting.' And I dart away before he recovers.

We have no ruse to lure him up there. We don't need one. I know he won't be able to resist.

It is dusk. Cia and I climb the mountain in a solemn procession. Cia bears the beer aloft behind me. She is frowning and I tell her not to poke her tongue out of the corner of her mouth like that, but the beer keeps spilling over the brim. I

205

carry the matches. We arrive at the glade, but it is not the same one as before. The Msasa trees have had a late budding and their boughs, which stroke one another in the wind, are wreathed in delicate leaves. They shade a garden of Eden, and though the freshly disturbed earth beneath which Moosejaw lies is still discernible, his grave feels peaceful. Then I notice the small withered posies on his burial mound. There are three – sorry little bunches of exotic and wild flowers that have obviously been deliberately picked and placed on the grave. Cia has been here before, it seems. I hope that Moosejaw has been watching when I have not.

We kneel down beside the grave. Cia leans over and ceremoniously places the gourd at its foot – a little of the fermenting beer dribbles over the rim – and then, with her hands, she brushes the ground around it clear of twig and pod debris. She wipes her dirtied hands on her dungarees and looks expectantly at me. I hesitate for a moment, not sure what to do next. Then I set to work creating a little mound of kindling and strike a match to it. I am fearful of starting a fire now, after everything, but the *murombo* seems to need one. The kindling smoulders and the edges of the leaves burn crimson and shrivel and we kneel there watching our offering as the embers die. It is time to perform the blessing.

We each dip our fingers into the beer and, rising, sprinkle it in a circle around Moosejaw's grave, chanting, 'Ashes to ashes, dust to dust. Peace be with you.' It is holy, a holy incantation, culled from one of the few times we went to mass. It seems fitting. We say it over and over again. Then, to finish, I make the sign of the cross. Cia says, 'Ah men.' After finishing, we sit down next to the grave and wait for darkness and Ronin. I feel strangely calm now that the hour is nigh. The sacrament has worked. There is a feeling of sanctity about the place. The ground on which we sit is hallowed now.

A barred owl hoots way up in the trees above us, proclaiming that his hour has come and all this is his domain, but Cia hears something else.

'Nyree? Nyree, did you hear that? The owl called my name. Did you hear it?'

Slowly the waiting begins to strum on my innards. The sense of calm evaporates. I shiver as a chill descends, and from something other than the chill too, I think. I can tell Cia is nervous. Her hands that were still now twitch. I notice the crescents of grit under her nails.

'Do you think he'll come, Nyree?'

I am half hoping he won't. Twilight is fading.

Suddenly I hear something in the grove. A rustling. My belly flops over. I rake the trees with my eyes but I can't make out anything in the greyness. Then I see him, Ronin, sloping through the trees. As he emerges into the clearing, he stops and stares at us for a long moment. His beautiful, vacant face looks hungry. Then, almost imperceptibly, his lip curls into a sneer and I am afraid. I look down at Cia beside me and am even more afraid to see that she is not. The waiting over, her face is steely, as if she is ready.

Then Ronin draws a breath as if to speak, but he never gets the chance. Cia stands up first and I am taken aback. I watch her stand and speak to Ronin as if she's rehearsed it and I'm just the audience.

'Ronin, what you did was wrong.'

There is silence.

Then she draws a deep breath. 'It was wrong, okay, and nothing can change that. Moosejaw is dead and you killed him. But you can say you're sorry, and you can beg for forgiveness, and maybe, maybe Moosejaw will forgive you.'

Ronin half shakes his head, as if he doesn't believe what he's heard. Then he snorts and says, all contemptuously, 'You have got to be joking, right? You stupid, stupid little girls, why would I ever be sorry?'

Cia sighs. Then she fumbles in her dungarees pocket and pulls something out. I can't see what it is. She stares at it, then slowly turns her wrist to reveal it to Ronin. 'Because if you don't say sorry, I'll make you,' she replies, taking a deliberate step backwards. 'This is a picture of your grandfather and your mother, and it's all you'll ever have of them – your own family. So if you ever want to see this again, you say you're sorry now and for ever ah men.'

I can't believe it. Cia, all on her own, has gone and taken from Angélique's treasure trove the picture of Seamus with his daughter and is using it to blackmail Ronin. The hair on the nape of my neck bristles. It is too dangerous for Cia to play this game. She'll lose. Weaker, because she doesn't have a mind that twists like his. This blackmail is cunning but, even so, not cunning enough. I see her flourish the photos. She thinks she has the power. She can't see how vulnerable she is. I know she's doomed.

Ronin stares silently at Cia, then takes a step towards her. With that one step – nothing more, just a step – my gut lurches. Something has begun. I step aside as Cia leaps backwards over Moosejaw's grave and, with that, we are separated. Ronin takes another step towards her and another. She stays just out of reach, stepping backwards. They are slowly circling Moosejaw's grave, bound by it in some way.

Then Ronin's face contorts and he lunges at her, but Cia is too nimble for him. She darts out of his way. Ronin grunts.

'Give it to me,' he says hoarsely, lunging at her again.

'No,' Cia shouts jubilantly. 'You can't ever have it – not until you're sorry, truly sorry.'

For a moment she looks angelic. A celestial light is all around her – she is lit from within. In her veins pumps the blood of Jan Christiaan – he, too, was lit from within by the fires of a holy mission. I know that this is what she needed. Then she dances away through the trees. Ronin stumbles after her, and I, as though in a trance, follow them: the angel and her hunter.

Cia is prancing down the mountain along the banks of the stream that tumbles through a slight fissure on the mountain face. The woods that thread its banks are dank and tangled. A filigree of creepers trails down from half-rotting boughs and the undergrowth of ferns and mosses is slick and luscious. The pale bladder of the moon bathes everything in an ethereal light. The air is tinged with the raw smell of damp earth churned up by worms and the probing fungus fingers that suck life out of death, the smell of the forest that lives for ever. Cia is flitting through trees, leaping over boulders and fallen logs. A lissom wood seraph. Ronin is behind her, crashing through the forest with none of the seraph's nimbleness. I am only a few paces behind him but it seems to me that he is nevertheless gaining on her.

'Cia!' I call. To warn her. But she doesn't hear me. She doesn't even glance backward as she dances through the weeping willows. Night has drained the colour from the woods, hulking shapes loom black around me, night creatures screech to find one another. Ronin is possessed of something feral – he has become one of them as he tears through the woods below me.

I am too far behind them. I am trying to keep up, but I keep stumbling over knobbly roots and rocks. Every time I near Ronin, I reach out, grabbing feebly at him. He doesn't even look back at me. Then I stagger and lose him again.

Something changes. I sense it the moment it does. Maybe she heard him behind her, heard his ragged breath – she didn't know how close he was – and in an instant, the dance is over. He hunts her. She knows she is the hunted. I am on the outside, watching. She is no longer prancing, fleet of foot – she's running, running for her life. Vines now claw at her, roots twist and buckle to snare her feet. I hear her panting, panting. I, too, am out of breath: the air singes my lungs. I can smell the hunt: the fear of the hunted, the lust of the hunter. No one makes a sound on the flight down the mountain in the ghost light; there is just the smell and the knowledge. This is a hunt to the death.

Maybe she knew she couldn't outrun him, that he was gaining on her, getting closer and closer; she was hidden beneath an old fallen tree, in its skirts of moss and ferns. He has seen her. The quarry. He lets out a scream of triumph. She bolts out from under him, panicky, desperate now. She flees before him.

I glance up from my own precarious flight in time to see Cia leap on to a large boulder, a roughly hewn square, jutting over the edge of the stream. It must be slimy with water and algae, and as her foot lands on it, it slides out from under her. She teeters for a moment on the edge. In the seconds that she falters, trying not to lose her balance, Ronin closes in on her. He comes to a jarring halt, blocking the way back at the edge of the boulder. Cia turns and realizes she is trapped. There is terror on her face. She looks up behind him and sees me skidding down the slope towards them.

'Nyree, help me!' she cries.

I look around desperately, then bend down and grab a rock. Ronin looks over his shoulder and sees me poised to hurl it into the back of his skull. 'Get back!' he snarls.

His snarl grips my bowels. I waver. He turns again and charges towards Cia. She is desperate. There is no way out for her. The granite is treacherous. Below its jagged edge the stream cascades over a little ridge; I hear the rushing of the waterfall in the silence.

Cia raises her head to me. 'Nyree! Please!'

Ronin turns once more. He looks me in the eyes. His are deadly cold, and I quail inside. The rock stays in my hand. Ronin turns and, as if in slow motion, lunges towards Cia and tries to grab her. Cia flails backwards but she is already on the edge. She falls.

I cry out once. '*Cia!*'

Ronin freezes. I thrust past him and run the few paces down to just below the granite boulder. The water pools there in a shallow basin below the little waterfall where Cia is lying face up just under the water. I draw a tattered breath before falling to my knees in the water beside her.

It is strange: she is beautiful, serene, floating there beneath the watery film, her eyes half closed, her hair streaming around her head. Beside her the pictures of Ronin's mother and her dead father spin madly, snagged on the water eddies. For a moment I am in the attic with its dim stone walls, billowing with shadows and the cold breath of ancestors. Then a voice howls inside me, 'No! She can't breathe!'

I plunge my hands into the water to lift her head, and as I bend forward I see it. My fingers have strayed into a cloud around her head that I hadn't noticed before in the half-light. Blood is staining the water in the darkness. Before I have even recovered to lift her from the water, I know. I know from her utter stillness and the dark stain of the blood in the water. No one I know is looking out from those eyes.

I know it absolutely. And then I scream. I scream from my guts – it is wrenched out of me from deep down – and it comes out raw, bestial. It goes on and on, tasting of bile and blood. It echoes down into the valley, and soon I see lights flickering in the woods below, and as it peters out into sobs, I hear voices calling. While we are still alone, I look up to see Ronin standing lifeless at the edge of the pool. His face is the soul of horror. And then he runs.

Moments later Mom and Jobe crash through the trees, carrying lights and shotguns. After that, the terrible slow-motion clarity dissolves and everything becomes fragmented and confused.

21

They think she is only unconscious – she will wake up and she will be fine. She can't have drowned; she was only under water for a moment. And her wound, the cut to the back of her head, is nothing; it is an ugly gash right at the base of her skull, but still, just a glancing blow she caught as she slipped and fell.

They pick up her limp body, which I am still cradling, and lay her on the bank. They kneel over her and give her the kiss of life, but once they understand that the reason she isn't breathing isn't because her lungs are waterlogged, they cease trying to revive her and, staunching the blood that still seeps from the wound as best they can – ripping the hem from Mom's cotton nightdress – they carry her swiftly down to the farmhouse.

I can no longer speak. I don't even know how I made them understand what happened – that she fell, hitting her head on the rock before she went into the water – but once I had it no longer mattered. I was forgotten. They take Cia away from me and carry her off into the night. I stumble blindly after them, tears still searing my eyeballs and the back of my throat, but silently now. By the time I reach the farmhouse they've laid Cia on the couch in the front room. Oupa is there, too, now and is trying to wake her. The generator has died and she is lit by dozens of candles and oil lamps. In the soft glow they cast she is rosy, yet still she will not wake. Mom holds two fingers to Cia's wrist. I see her eyes get panicky – like little birds, they dart about – but you can't tell from her voice.

'We must get her to a doctor. Quickly.'

Mom snatches up the keys to the old Landie – I see her hands are trembling now – and runs out. Jobe follows, carrying Cia's lifeless body out of the front door to the revving vehicle. They roar off into the night, Mom, Jobe and Oupa, leaving me with Blessing in the aftermath, in the silence, on death watch. Ronin has not returned.

I keep my lonely, silent vigil for hours. I think about the flying doctor while I wait. Me and Cia love the advert on TV for him: 'Is it a bird? Is it a plane? No! It's the Flying Doctor!' We've done it loads of times on the lawn. When we get to the part about it not being a bird but the Flying Doctor, we swoop down out of the sky to save sick people on faraway farms. Where is he tonight? Why did they have to drive off into the darkness? I have no answers but I keep asking questions like that because they make me feel nice and numb.

Finally they return. The Landie's engine gasps and dies, its lights dim and go out. I realize I've been holding my breath, hoping when I know there's no hope. They mount

216

the steps, bowed. Cia is no longer with them. It is that simple thing – just her being gone – that fills me with such a feeling of emptiness I think I'm going to suffocate; there's no air. A hole yawns inside me and I ache.

'Nyree. Nyree, come here to me,' says Mom, sounding strangled. She kneels down and reaches her arms towards me. I watch her warily.

'Nyree, your sister . . . Cia . . . I . . . Cia is . . .' She chokes on her words.

She tries to take me in her arms but I wrench free and flee.

I don't want to stay in our bedroom either. Tonight will be only the second time that Cia isn't sleeping next to me in it. The other time was long, long ago. Cia went to hospital to have an operation. The hospital was called the Salisbury Central. I was taken to visit her in the children's ward. I remember her toddling towards me down the centre of the black and white chequered aisle between the ranks of sterile metal cots and starched white linen. I was jealous of her, but she was so pleased to see me that I forgave her. I remember it in the fragmented way you remember the earliest things, mainly because it was the first time that I understood Cia was separate from me, was not me, could go places I couldn't go, could know things I didn't know. Alone now in our room, without Cia to smother whispers with and pretend not to be scared of the dark for, I don't know what to do. We were still one after all, and with her gone, I am no more.

*

I drag my way through the next few days as if a weight around my neck is towing me down. Dad came home the day after. There is a haggard air about him and a look in his eyes – I have seen it before in the eyes of the animals who are caught in the snares laid about the farm by poachers, or at least those that are still alive when we find them: bewildered, wounded. The dead ones have the glassy look that Oupa now wears. He sits mute on the *stoep*, grimly drinking gin after gin until he slips into a fitful doze, a thin sliver of drool hanging from his half-agape mouth. Mom tries hard for my sake, or maybe for her own. She may as well not bother. I am breathing inside a thick membrane. Nothing can pierce it. I am inside looking out, not really there, deadened.

I go to the funeral in my thick membrane. The church is in Umtali. We drive there in the Peugeot. I have to sit carefully on the back seat – I am not allowed to get my black velvet pinafore crumpled. It's new, specially for Cia's funeral. I wipe the skirt out smooth from under me and perch on it, trying not to get any crumples in it. The church is groaning with people. We walk down the aisle past them. Mom holds my hand all the way to the front pew, which is left empty for us, the most important people in the church. Oupa, Dad and Ronin walk behind us. I stare straight ahead, not looking at the people who aren't as important as us. A priest in a frilly black dress with a doily round his neck starts to speak. I don't look either at the small casket before the altar. It's close by, too close. I feel it. Cia is awake for her funeral, though. She is surprised at being dead. Also, she's anxious to help small creatures in trouble. She's indignant at the injustice of

218

it. She shows me the big cross above the altar with Jesus Christ hanging on it with his headdress of thorns, dripping blood everywhere and looking miserable, because he's busy dying even though he's saving us from our sins.

Mom said the funeral is to say goodbye to Cia, but I don't want to do that. The priest in his frilly dress is still talking and talking. He says we must give thanks to Jesus for taking Cia for himself. I hate Jesus. What do they mean He rose from the dead? How exactly? Was it in some flimsy, unsatisfactory way, like a ghost? Ghosts are like memories or dreams; thin and frail and fleeting. Cia only goes to sleep when the coffin slides through the little velvet curtains of the crematorium. She touched the silk lining of her coffin softly between her fingertips and went to sleep. I know she won't ever wake again.

On the way out I see Jobe standing at the back of the church. We walk in a slow procession behind the priest down the aisle past the pews where everyone is sitting except Jobe, who stands right at the back of the church by the door. He is wearing a black suit. The sleeves are too short and he holds his trilby in his hands and snot and tears are gushing down his face. It seems strange to see tears leaking out of Jobe's eyes like that.

Afterwards, I see Dell and Damian and the others in the churchyard. They are all there, huddled under the archway that leads out to the cemetery. They stare at me with a new look. It is horror mixed with awe. I am different now, set apart. I feel self-conscious under the stares. There are others like me: Louis and André's mom was killed accidentally when she trod on a landmine on their farm. That was before their dad moved them to town. André doesn't remember his mom. Louis does, though. He says he remembers that she smelled nice. And one kid in KG2 had a brother who drowned in their reservoir. I feel them looking at me, too. The ones who know. The rest stare at me with their new look. Before, I was just another kid, and now I'm changed, above them, no longer one of them.

I haven't thought of him. Ronin. I try not to. It's like he isn't there and like he was never there. Not all the time, though. Sometimes I've seen him out of the corner of my eye, hovering, just on the edge of my vision, at the edge of my thoughts. At the funeral he sat on the other side of Mom and Dad and I never even looked at him. But now I have to think of him. I'm sitting in the dining room, at the high table. Dad is sitting opposite me, waiting. He asked me what happened. No one's asked me before now, no one, not once. I don't know why. But now, after the funeral, after the saying goodbye to Cia, Dad wants to know why. I don't know how to answer.

Why were we up there at night? What in God's name were we doing? How did Cia fall?

I don't know where to begin. Looking back, it feels as though we were on a spiral staircase. One thing just led to another, until we were almost falling down it, going faster and faster, and none of us could stop, could change things, could go back. So I start at the end.

'We went to Moosejaw's grave. We went to do a *murombo* to cleanse it of evil spirits. Ronin got angry and he went after

Cia. She was running from him and she fell. That was it. It's like Ronin was the evil spirit all along.'

I speak in a flat voice, but I hate him. I hate him with a hatred so powerful it constricts my breathing. My chest heaves. Dad doesn't understand. He frowns, shakes his head. Then everything gushes out of me – everything that happened since the day Ronin came to the Vumba. I know I've spat out the stale fear and anger, but my guilt I secrete inside me. I don't tell him what happened at the end. That she begged me to save her, that I failed her, that I saved myself, curdles inside my belly. I tell Dad only what I need to to condemn Ronin.

'Jesus. I didn't see it. But he's only a boy, Amy, a boy.'

But I know Mom blames Ronin.

Oupa sits and stares. Then he says quietly, over and over, that it's his fault Cia's dead. 'I never should have made Angélique give up that baby.'

Mom and Dad aren't listening to this gibbering old man. It's apparent they know this story. I don't, but I don't care.

'But it was just after the war, a hell of a homecoming after all those years. I forgave her – she was so lonely, and God help me I loved her – but him . . . You can never forgive a brother's betrayal. I just couldn't stand the sight of that baby girl . . .' He sinks into himself.

I watch and wait. They can't bear him, any of them, they want him out. Gone. There are trunk calls. They are trying to find his mother again, but she is not to be found. Then there are calls to the school, to the headmaster. Dad says money will have to change hands, but he'll do what it takes.

They drive him out of Modjadji's front gates. I don't feel happy, though. I feel nothing. Instead I see again what I saw that night: the look in his eyes. Horror. Was he sorry for what he'd done? If he was, the sorrow was already corrupted by something mean and shabby: fear. We shared that.

Oupa always says our fate is written by our characters. So it was with Cia, and so it is with Ronin. It is only now that Cia is dead that I understand that Ronin is only half alive, that something inside *him* is dead, and looking down the road, as the car shrinks into a cloud of dust, at the years stretching ahead of him, I'm glad that everywhere he goes, Ronin will always take himself.

22

Time passes slowly now. It has a greyness about it and it is sluggish and numb. I watch Mom and Dad through the numbness. Dad is angry. It is like he is imprisoned in anger. It's always there, the anger, rippling just underneath his skin. His skin barely holds it in – I can feel it seeping out of the pores. He makes me nervous now. I stay out of his way. I feel sorry for the Afs, though – they can't get out of his way. If they do anything wrong, and they always do something wrong, Dad hollers at them something awful. His eyes go all bulgy in their sockets, and flecks of spit fly out of his mouth and he hollers at them about having pig shit for brains and being bone idle and whatnot.

He doesn't holler at Mom, though, and somehow the not-hollering is worse. At suppertime we sit in silence, the sound of silver scraping on old china too loud. Sometimes Mom says something pretend, like how hot it is for the time of year and how she's feeling faint from the heat. Dad says nothing, and how hot it is and her going to faint just dangles there in the air. There's nothing but sawing and chewing and swallowing for a while, and then she says something sharp and pointy: 'Sean? Don't you agree? I mean, it's obvious you couldn't care less how I'm feeling, but surely you're suffering the heat?'

Dad grunts something with no words but which means shut up – warning her. Oupa, soaked in gin, barely says anything as he drools and guzzles his way through the meal. His false teeth are loose on his gums and he sucks little hunks of meat instead of chewing them. A ring of sucked-out meat chunks grows on the rim of his plate. Mom says he masticates and says he's disgusting and how his disgustingness grates on her nerves. Oupa carries on drooling and guzzling and says your mother's become a bloody martyr.

Then Mom sighs and says, in a clipped voice, 'Sean, I realize that boorishness is your mainstay, these days, but do you think it would be possible for you at least to *try* to be civil just for dinner this evening.'

I know she does it on purpose. Dad's head snaps up so hard he'll give himself whiplash and he throws her a mean look, so mean it makes my stomach twist. Then he deliberately scrapes his chair back across the slate floor and stalks out. Mom sighs like it's put upon her to suffer and says, 'Come along, Nyree, finish your meal.'

It's worse, too, when they don't fight. Then the silence sits between them like a third person. A stranger. Swollen. Poisonous. Mom locks the door to their bedroom at night. Sometimes I hear them screaming at each other before she shuts him out. I climb out of my bed and creep down the passage and listen outside their door like a sneak. Through the thick walls and heavy wooden door, I hear only snatches – when Mom's voice goes shrill. I can't hear him well, his voice is too low, but I know when she's got him. That's when he says nothing at all and I have to run because I know I have only a few moments before he wrenches open the door and storms downstairs and out of the house.

'Why don't I just leave and you can find a new slave for yourself and your miserable, whingeing father?'

That's her when her voice goes all shrill.

'Jesus, Amy, I was just trying to say that you don't seem to be coping too well, all right?'

I know that wasn't all he was saying – he wasn't saying it to be nice anyway.

'But if you feel that way, maybe I'll go and let's see how well you cope without me busting my fucking chops to keep food on the table and a roof over our heads.'

'No, no, I don't know what we'll do without your genius for screaming at natives, your crude language and foul temper, but don't worry too much at least on one score – I doubt your daughter will miss you terribly. It's not like you've been a father or anything to her all these years.'

She seems to know just what to pick on and how to do it. She has that instinct. Behind their bed she's stuck a little card that says: 'Along the way, take time to smell the roses.' On it a little mouse is sniffing a daisy.

225

Later, I hear her weeping. In the morning, Dad is cold, pitiless; Mom is soaked in wretchedness. After he leaves, she stands and stares glassily out of the window.

'Mom? Are you okay, Mom?' I whisper.

It irritates her. 'It's . . . it's nothing. Never mind.' Her voice quivers.

She stumbles blindly on through her day, deaf, too, to anything but the voices in her head. She hisses back at them sometimes. I catch her hissing and spitting at them while staring into nowhere.

I hate being around them – his hostile eyes, her self-pity, the way she punishes him. And all of it, the screaming, the crying, the silences, to drown her out: the ghost who hovers in the air around us.

Oupa drowns her out with gin. He has surrendered completely to it – like he wants it to destroy him – and no one even tries to stop him. The way Mom watches him, half disgusted, half satisfied, it feels almost as if she wants it to destroy him too, wants him to destroy himself. It hasn't taken long: he's like an old scarecrow, whose clawlike hands tremble uncontrollably, whose bloodshot eyes see only into the past and who soils himself.

I don't care. I'm too tired to care. Tiredness has seeped into me, seeped deeply into my bones and all the way to the deep, secret place inside me. Even breathing makes me tired, weary. Mostly I just climb into the fork of a huge spreading marula tree down by the riverine and spend the whole day lying in it. I don't think about Cia, I don't think

226

about her dying, I don't even miss her: the tiredness has sapped me of all feeling.

Only at night do I stir. It began the night after she died and now every night, in the dark, after I close my eyes, I see it, from the insides of my eyeballs, always the same: fire and a black pit. Cia and Moosejaw have come back from the dead, and over and over Cia tries to save him. She never does. She calls his name, she tries to reach him, in her hand she clutches a withered posy, but Moosejaw always ends up in the pit, fire raging above him. He looks up at me as I look down at him, but I can't help him, and then the tongues of flame are licking him and smoke boils over him and I can see him no more. Then I see Cia floating beneath her watery grave. I kneel over her and, as I do so, her eyes fly open and I wake. I am drenched in sweat and breathing hard. Sometimes, as her eyes open, Cia's hand comes out of the water and she grasps my wrist. I feel the pressure of her fingers. When I wake, I hear the walls whispering to me. They hiss and cackle like static; my curtains billow gently though my sash windows are shut fast. I look down and watch the little red dimples fade to white.

In a way it is only in the dreams that I am still alive, that I feel anything at all. And what I feel is fear. Once my heart stops hammering in my chest and the fear has faded, for a moment I feel a sadness so deep that it's going to pull me under and drown me. Then I shut down and the long dullness of the day begins.

And that is how time goes by, with a dull film to blunt the day and terror by night.

227

Then one day I walk into Mom and Dad's bedroom and find Mom sitting on the floor surrounded by a sea of pictures. The pictures scare me: Cia grins happily out from hundreds of them. Mom is crying softly. I stand there in the doorway uncertainly, listening to her cry in the sea of Cia, but when she looks up, I see that she is smiling through her tears.

I'm hanging upside-down off the bed next to her on the floor and we're gorging on the photos and we're really together, she's really here and she really sees me and I'm basking in it, in her seeing me. Mom says the pictures are an opiate. Cia smiles like a Cheshire cat.

Dad walks into the room and stops hard and I think he's going to rip the pictures right out of our hands and tear them up. He lashes out with his arm – he's going to slap Mom. But he doesn't. His arm just flays the air and he makes a guttural noise in his throat. Then he kneels down and picks up a photo. It's Cia with the chameleon perched on her head at Mermaid's Pool. Standing under a huge tree, dripping wet in her glorious orange bikini bottom, she is looking up at me a little to her side, her expression painfully self-conscious. Dad stares at it for a long moment. Then he clutches it to his breast, bows low and starts to sob.

Things are better now. Dad's anger has dissolved, his rippling skin has sagged and he doesn't holler at the Afs any more, but he's not quite the same either. There are shadows around his eyes now. When he comes home from fighting he doesn't do the ambush. I see the shadows and I know he'll never be the same again.

Mom is going to save Oupa. He needs saving from himself.

'There's a kind of vanity in guilt, Patrick, in tenderly nursing it, a simpering self-pity in despising yourself.'

Oupa is none too grateful. Mom makes him take his *muti* and he's not allowed to pull his false teeth out any more and he has to eat chicken soup, and Oupa says her bellyaching at him is enough to drive a man to drink and how he himself has a bellyache from the peace she's destroyed and I know that maybe even Oupa is going to be all right. Mom puts the picture of Cia at Mermaid's Pool up on the mantelpiece. Great-grandfather's ghostly eyes watch over her.

Some of the magic is gone, though. The fairies have withered and died, their wings crunchy like dragonflies'. Now glow-worms are just glow-worms glowing faintly under bushes at night.

23

And now we have lost it all, of course. Those are her words, Mom's, her voice crisp and brittle. It's Comrade Mugabe who's taken it. I saw him on TV, swearing an oath. There is going to be peace and freedom now. Dad says his speech was a bunch of Cold War rhetoric. The air is charged with static and some of the farm Afs eye Dad with a new resentfulness.

Mom and Dad sat me down at the dinner table and warned me not to say anything against our new leaders at school and made me cross my heart and hope to die if I ever repeat anything Oupa has to say about them. Spies are everywhere, you see – your own neighbour could inform on you. At least, that's what they said, but I knew it wasn't likely to be our own neighbour, no, it was more likely to be Gaddaffi. Gaddaffi was in my class at school and his father is a local Rabble-rouser. Gaddaffi was chauffeur-driven to school in a sleek black Mercedes limousine. Me and Dell were most impressed. Even if it wasn't Gaddaffi who informed on you, it could be any one of the other black kids who came to our school since Independence allowed them to Darken its Portals. Trust no one. But behind their backs, we called them the Non-swimmers and laughed at their belly-buttons that bulged out of their cozzies, until soon they outnumbered us, and Mom and Dad took me away from the school for Non-swimmers.

In my new school, I don't have to sing the song of the new names for every place in the country, 'Salisbury-Harare! Victoria-Masvingo!' and on and on, but they're changing anyway, and the statues of Livingstone and Rhodes and Selous were toppled, and the flag was remade in the colours of the fight for freedom, and now we don't sing 'Rise O Voices of Rhodesia' in assembly any more. Now we sing '*Nkosi Sikelel' iAfrica*'.

At one of the roadblocks that have sprouted on the way into town the policeman studies Dad's papers for a long time. He narrows his eyes and peers closely at suspicious bits. Then he rifles through the car's boot with surly relish. His subordinate looks on with interest, his gun aimed casually at Dad's belly. Then he slams the boot, beams at me and asks if we don't have a Coke for the thirsty work. Indeed, sweat stains spread alarmingly from under his armpits.

Dad burned his army uniform and the old Rhodesian flag that hung on the wall behind the bar counter next to the brass elephant clock. We had a big bonfire down by the compost heap. Dad doused it with petrol, and acrid smoke billowed over us as all the years of fighting were cremated. He hid his shiny badge and medals in the attic, though. Mom called him a sentimental old bugger and said he was courting trouble. If he noticed the years of dust disturbed by two sets of small footprints and one of paws, he said nothing.

There are rumours leaking out of Matabeleland in the south. Rumours about the people being massacred. Jobe heard them and wrung his hands, but the radio told only about the peace and the freedom and denounced the racist enemies of the state who are trying to subvert it with their lies and treachery. And then, one day, a letter came.

It was written in the beautiful, ornate hand of a mission-school-taught scribe and it told of the murder of the last of his family by people called the Fifth Brigade. The women were shamed, the *induna* tortured, his village razed. They were buried in a mass grave it said; men, women and children, riddled with bullets. Jobe wept.

After that, we got the expropriation order, which means that the government is taking your house. It is going to be Confiscated. The government man in a dark suit came with a lot of AK47-toting teenagers in a battered old army truck. They strutted about with their AKs and Dad called the man 'sir' and sort of bowed to him a lot and then he signed a paper. In the end, none of us has to bear Great-grandfather's legacy – Cia is dead and now the legacy too, has died, after it fell upon us to pay for his ill-gotten gains. I think of Great-grandfather sometimes, with his soulless eyes, his blood, sweat and tears that watered the earth.

Later, Mom, Dad and Oupa watched the sunset from the *stoep* and then got drunk late into the night on Great-grandfather's collection of vintage wines. Most of them were bad – corked, they said. I sat at the top of the stairs, my legs and arms stuck through the banister, listening to them.

'Oh, well, can't say we didn't have a good innings, though, hey? But the day of the *mukiwa* is done,' Dad said, to no one in particular.

Oupa nodded sagely.

'Yup,' said Dad, cheerfully drunk. 'It's hell in Africa, man. Cheers!'

Oupa and Mom joined in the toast with gusto, clinking their crystal, and swigging the bad corked wine.

'*Pamberi chongwe!*' bellowed Oupa, as he slammed his glass down on the table.

But it was the last time Oupa did anything with gusto. It was as if he couldn't leave the land, the place of his ancestors. He shrank before he died. I pitied him, when pity was the last thing he'd have wanted. Towards the end, he just faded away from the world. The memory of the very old is a rubbish heap of trivia – a quarrel with a servant, a hunt for a lost dog, the expression on a long-dead brother's face, the rain lashing down on a stormy afternoon seventy years ago. Anything that really matters is outside their range of vision.

In his last hours he recovered some his old feistiness, and I do swear it was the priest summoned to his deathbed, oddly by Dad, who revived him.

'He maketh me to lie down in green pastures: He leadeth me beside still waters. He restoreth my soul: He leadeth me in the paths of the righteous for his name's sake.'

The words were beautiful, mysterious, soothing as water.

'Yea, though I walk through the valley of the shadow of

death,' intoned the crimson-faced young cleric, 'I shall fear no evil.'

'I plan ter run, meself,' muttered Oupa.

'Do not mock, sir. You have no time for mockery – the end is nigh.'

Oupa chuckled. 'That's true. And surely goodness and mercy shall follow me these last days of my life.'

I crouched in the corner of the room when Jobe came to pay his last respects. He stood solemnly by Oupa's deathbed, his battered old trilby in his hands, and offered him the succour of his own god: 'Eh, Baba, my God, He lives above. He is a pool of water in the sky. My God He is a rain-bringer, a giver of life. I come to my God through my ancestors, my *amadlozi*. I give praise to my God and I dance. My *amadlozi* are with me always and the voice of my God comes from within, from the beginning of time. He is in the earth, in the roots of the trees. Eh, Baba, do you want to know my God?'

'That god, *umkhulu*,' chuckled Oupa, 'that is the god I already know.'

Jobe inclined his head.

'Well, old man, I'm at the end of one and 'tis time for me to take a new journey.'

'*Eh-heh*, I know this,' agreed Jobe.

'Things are changing,' said Oupa. 'My time is over. The natives are restless.'

'*Yebo*, Baba, the young ones are restless.'

It was I who saw him last. I hovered in the doorway of the room in which he lay, choked by the sight of him staring listlessly up at the mouldy ceiling, panting reedily. He stirred when I entered and took his hand in mine.

'It was such a lovely day, I thought it a pity to get up,' he quipped.

I smiled.

He smiled back at me for a long moment. 'Don't let it end like this,' he said, 'tell them I said something.'

And that was it. I could make more of it, but that would be a lie. The truth is that Oupa died shrivelled. There was little left of who he once was, of the world in which he lived. He took even the memory of it with him, and his death was almost a relief to those of us he left behind. Only those self-ishly seized by the gods before their time live on eternally young, beautiful, all that they could have been, unmarred by failure, for ever missed by those who loved them.

And now the house is empty, our life in crates, the rooms of Great-grandfather's citadel already echoing with our ghosts. The animals have been auctioned off, the farm workers evicted, their pleading, '*Eh*, Baas! *Eh*, Baas, what about the job, Baas? My children are hungry, Baas!' still ringing in my ears. It stands bare, but for the debris of an evacuation. The dust hangs in the air of the empty feed warehouse where we used to jump on the sacks of *mielies*; the algae that clung to the walls of the drained reservoirs hasn't yet dried and flaked off; and a strip of wet *biltong* swings forlornly in the slaughterhouse.

Slowly I climb the creaking staircase and at last find myself in the attic chamber, our attic, Cia's and mine and

236

Moosejaw's. And Angélique's. It has been stripped up here too and it is as dim and shadowy as ever, but the light seeping through the stained, leaded-glass pane in the window feels enchanted. I stand in the dusty silence and listen.

I look down at the metal box I've carried up in my hand. It is one of Oupa's old tobacco tins, blue, rusting around the rim, a ship sailing to nowhere on the lid. We each had one once, Cia and I, treasure boxes, little troves of luck. I prise open the lid and finger the artefacts inside it, each still imbued with magic, gritty with memories: a tooth, a warthog tusk, a penny from the Imperial Rhodesian mint, one of Grover's eyes plucked off by Moosejaw, an engraved silver pillbox stolen from Ouma's trousseau with a lucky bean and a guinea-fowl tail feather inside. Below is a crumpled photograph of the dead – a man cradling his baby daughter – faded and stained with water and sorrow and, crouching in the corner, a shrivelled scarab corpse with a tiny stake pierced through its horn. I hadn't known it was there. Kneeling there on the floor, I wonder why Cia hid her amulet in my box. But there is no time now for wondering. I press the lid back on, shimmy up on to one of the low, pitched rafters and stash my box behind the crossbeam.

Now I have nothing left to do. I traipse through Modjadji's husk, leaves littering the corners and fireplaces, and I see her in the years ahead. Left unbridled, the Zimbabwe creeper that always sought to strangle the pillars stationed along the front *stoep* has garotted its whole edifice – thick ropes of knotted vines trail down from the support beams. The house has aged. It has shrunk, of course, but more than that, our desertion has weakened it against time, sapped it of its grit. It is still heralded by the Cape Dutch gable, but the roof behind it has sagged and the walls are pockmarked with bullet holes.

Outside the kitchen door I find that Jobe has made tea and peanut butter and jam sandwiches for me one last time. I sit on the flagstone steps squashing the layers of bread between my palms, listening to the distant sounds of the revving Landie and the commotion of a trailer-towing tractor as it trundles up to the warehouse – a gang of Afs is perched atop, whistling and braying abuse at their driver as he attempts inexpertly to reverse up to the loading bay. I look down and see Cia sitting on the step below me. Somehow I'm not surprised.

I smile at her, then solemnly peel one half of my sandwich and slowly lick out the filling. She smiles back – shy, smug, irrepressibly pleased with herself. The memory of that Cheshire-cat smile, having taken so long to find, inflicts an intimate pain. I close my eyes against it and feel Cia's hot, sticky hand in mine.

Glossary

Abelungu	white people (Zulu/Ndebele, plural of stem *-lungu*)
Af(s)	black African(s) (Rhodesian slang, abbreviation of African)
Ag	exclamation (Afrikaans slang, no direct translation)
Amadlozi	ancestral spirits (Zulu/Ndebele, plural of stem *-dlozi*)
Amaphoyisa	police (Zulu)
Baas	boss (African slang)
Baba	father (Zulu/Ndebele, polite form of address for an older man)
Bayede	hail (Zulu/Ndebele, respectful greeting for members of the royal house)
Biltong	strips of cured beef or venison (Afrikaans)
Bi-scope	cinema (Rhodesian English)
Bloed-vermenging	blood mingling (Afrikaans)
Boere orkes	farmers' ensemble (Afrikaans)

Boer	farmer (Afrikaans)
Braai	barbecue (Afrikaans, abbreviation of *braai vleis*: grilled meat)
Broekies	panties (Afrikaans slang, derivation of *broeke*, meaning pants or trousers)
Bundu	remote areas (Rhodesian slang)
Bushveld	wild terrain (South African slang)
Charf	pretend (South African slang)
Eina	exclamation (generic slang, no direct translation)
Eish	exclamation (generic Bantu language slang, no direct translation)
Eiwe	you (Rhodesian slang, derogatory form of address for a black African)
Flatdogs	crocodiles (Rhodesian slang)
Gijima	run (Zulu/Ndebele)
Gogo	grandmother (Zulu/Ndebele, pronounced with a soft *g*)
Gogos	bugs (Rhodesian slang, pronounced with a guttural *g*)
Gammadoolahs	remote areas (Rhodesian slang)
Hamba	go (Zulu/Ndebele)
'Hamba lusa! Hamba fasa!'	'Make looser! Make tighter!' ('Chilapalapa' dialect)
Hau	exclamation (generic Bantu language slang, no direct translation)

Idlozi	ancestral spirit (Zulu/Ndebele, singular of stem *-dlozi*)
Ijele	jail (Zulu)
Impi	army (Zulu)
Indaba	affair (Zulu/Ndebele)
Induna	headman or chief (Zulu/Ndebele)
Ingane	child (Zulu/Ndebele)
Inja	dog (Zulu/Ndebele)
Izimayini	mines (Zulu)
Ja	yes (Afrikaans)
Jislaaik	exclamation (Afrikaans slang, no direct translation)
Kaffir	black African (literally, infidel, derogatory)
Kapenta	local name for the introduced fish species *Alestes alestes* in Lake Tanganyika
Kaylite	polystyrene (Rhodesian slang)
Khaya	house, home (Zulu/Ndebele, stem of *ikhaya*)
Koeksusters	sweet plaited dough delicacy (Afrikaans, literally, baked sisters)
Kraal	corral (South African slang)
Lang-arm	long arm (Afrikaans slang, long-arm dancing)
Lobola	bride price (Zulu/Ndebele)

Legotlo	rat (northern Sotho)
Madala	old man (Zulu/Ndebele)
Makhulus	grandmothers (Zulu)
Mama	mother (Zulu/Ndebele, polite form of address for an older woman)
Maningi	plenty (Rhodesian slang from Zulu/Ndebele stem -*ningi*)
Mielies	maize (Southern African English/Afrikaans)
Mielie-meal	maize meal (Southern African English)
Miggies	midges or gnats (Afrikaans slang)
Mombies	cattle (Rhodesian slang from the Shona word *mombes*)
Mossie	sparrow (Afrikaans)
Mudzimu	ancestral spirits (Shona)
Mukiwa	white person (Bantu slang, also meaning wild fig)
Munt(s)	black African(s) (from the Bantu language word, *umuntu*, meaning human, derogatory)
Murungu	white person (Shona)
Mush/mushi	very nice (Rhodesian slang)
Muti	medicine (Rhodesian slang from the Zulu/Ndebele word *umuthi*)
N'anga	witch-doctor or shaman (Shona)

Nkosi	king or chief (Zulu/Ndebele, address form of *inkosi*)
Oom	uncle (Afrikaans)
Ouma	grandmother (Afrikaans)
Oupa	grandfather (Afrikaans)
Ousies	nannies (Afrikaans slang)
Padkos	packed lunch (Afrikaans, literally, road food)
Panga	machete (East African in origin)
Picanin	child (Rhodesian slang, Portuguese in origin)
Plaas-jaapie	hillbilly (Afrikaans slang)
Predikant	preacher (Afrikaans)
Putsi fly	a large green fly that typically lays its eggs on damp clothing or linen causing myiasis or infestation with fly larvae
Sadza	maize meal (Shona, staple food in Southern Africa)
Sangoma	witch-doctor or shaman (Zulu/Ndebele)
Shebeen	illegal saloon (Zulu slang)
Shesha	hurry (Zulu/Ndebele)
Shongololo	giant African millipede (also spelled *chongololo*)
Shumba	beer (Rhodesian slang)
Sis	gross; how revolting (Afrikaans slang)

Sjambok	whip (Afrikaans)
Skou	show (Afrikaans)
Soet koekies	sweet spiced cookies (Afrikaans)
Sommer	sort of (Afrikaans slang)
Spaza shop	informal general trader (South African slang)
Sterek	very or very much (Rhodesian slang)
Stoep	veranda (Afrikaans)
Takkies	trainers (Rhodesian/South African slang)
Tokoloshe	a mythical creature (in which there is widespread belief across Southern Africa); brown, hairy and dwarflike in appearance; largely mischievous, but malevolent under the control of a witch
Troopies	Rhodesian army soldiers (Rhodesian slang)
Tsetse fly	a large brownish fly that feeds exclusively on blood; transmits a disease of the central nervous system commonly known as sleeping sickness through a parasite in its saliva
Ubudoda	manhood (Zulu/Ndebele)
Udokotela	doctor (Zulu)
Umfana	boy (Zulu/Ndebele)
Umkhulu	grandfather (Zulu/Ndebele, polite or respectful form)

Umlungu	white person (Zulu/Ndebele, singular of stem *-lungu*)
Umoya	soul (Zulu/Ndebele)
Umshini	machines (Zulu)
Vaderland	fatherland (Afrikaans)
Veld	wild terrain (South African slang, derivative of *bushveld*)
Voetsek	go away (Afrikaans slang, offensive)
Volk	people; nation (Afrikaans)
Volkskas	Community Chest, i.e. building society (Afrikaans)
Voorkamer	formal reception room (Afrikaans, literally, front room)
Wildebees	gnu (Afrikaans, literally, wild beast)
Yebo	yes (Zulu)